Annabella's Story

MARY JO SCHELL

Copyright © 2024 Mary Jo Schell
All rights reserved
First Edition

Fulton Books
Meadville, PA

Published by Fulton Books 2024

ISBN 979-8-88982-831-0 (paperback)
ISBN 979-8-88982-832-7 (digital)

Printed in the United States of America

Part 1

Annabella

Chapter 1

It was a crisp morning in February 1863 as Annabella, Bella to her family and friends, walked outside. Each day she awoke at 6:00 a.m., dressed for the morning, and went outside to meet with Big George. Bella always wore some sort of hat on her head during inspections, not fancy, just functional. George was a large, burly Negro man in charge of overseeing the remaining slaves on her family's plantation just outside Vicksburg, Mississippi. He was in his forties, six feet tall, and over 250 pounds with curly black hair. His skin was such a dark brown that it reminded Bella of a moonless night. George's dark-brown eyes showed the torment he had experienced during his younger life, but his deep, husky voice was upbeat and friendly today. Each day, they inspected the property to discuss what needed to be worked on that day and how the livestock and crops were doing.

The one-thousand-plus-acre Johnson Plantation was at a minimum of activity these days. They were almost two years into the war, and Bella at the tender age of seventeen was currently responsible for the family and their safety. Soon she would be eighteen and hoped this war would bring her family home and life could return to normal. Although Bella doubted anything would be the way it was before.

Bella's mother, Mrs. Mary Elizabeth Morgan Johnson, was born in England on January 20, 1822. She was such an elegant lady, 5'3" tall, petite, with hair the color of sunshine and eyes the color of a summer sky. They were such a pale blue that sometimes they shone like diamonds. She usually wore her hair in a twist pinned up in the back. This made her look older than she actually was but also more in control. Mary met Bella's father, Jonathan Samuel Johnson, in Vicksburg at the age of sixteen when her parents moved there from England. They married two years later. Now, her life was too difficult for her to deal with. Her husband and two oldest sons were gone fighting in a war she did not understand. Most of the slaves were gone, and both cousin Marie and Uncle Edwin had died. Bella knew her Mother was unable to process all that had happened. Her way to manage each day was to behave as she always had before. Mary taught her three youngest children proper grammar, proper manners, proper writing and reading skills, and an appreciation for music. She ran the household with the domestic slaves as her mother had taught her. Everything else she just didn't discuss.

Big George and Bella would walk the area around the house first. The house was centered on a seven-acre plot about one half mile from the main road. This area was known as the main grounds. There were fences surrounding the main grounds with wide gate openings on three sides. On the fourth side, it stopped on either side of the looped drive in front of the house. The Mississippi river was three miles west of the house with the rest of the buildings surrounding three sides of the main grounds. The working area of the plantation consisted of forty acres, and the balance of the Plantation were crop fields and patches of woods. The pair would walk and inspect the conditions immediately related to the house first; flower gardens, sides of the house for any needed repairs, the roof, the windows, and the two kitchens. Raymond was doing well keeping the flower gardens in good-enough shape for Mother. The roof would need repairs soon, and the windows needed to be cleaned. It was difficult to maintain the rose garden with its gazebo in the southwest corner of the main grounds. When possible, some time would be spent keeping the weeds from taking over the area, but it was in great need of attention.

The large Japanese garden with the pond designed for koi fish was in the northwest corner of the main grounds. Everyone, including the slaves, found this area very relaxing and peaceful. Everyone would do a little maintenance to keep this garden in its original shape. There were Japanese-painted ferns and dwarf Japanese junipers, Japanese maple trees, and several white stones, both large and small, to accent some of the plants and create pathways. Mother loved the blue and lavender water lilies and sitting on one of the three benches. Lastly, there was a small Japanese-style structure to hold supplies.

The northeast and southeast corners of the main grounds were open lawns and had been used for parties and summer events. Now they would tie the goats in different areas every few days to manage the grass. They had tried using the sheep, but they wandered too much and didn't do well tied up like the goats.

"Should we tie the goats over near that stand of trees?" Bella asked as she pointed toward the magnolia trees and peony bushes that lined the open lawns, marking the edge of the main grounds.

"Yes, Ms. Bella, over ther' and ther'," Big George said as he pointed to the near and far sides of the trees next to the gate leading to the stables.

Bella shook her head as she said, "Remember the sheep. Why do they do so well in their own pastures but are so hopeless for the main grounds?"

Big George responded very matter-of-factly, "Ms. Bella, sheep is stupid, goats is smart."

Bella smiled. She enjoyed Big George's thoughts on the world. Some of the buildings needed painting and some of the kitchen bricks needed repairing. The kitchen was more important, so it took priority.

The two kitchens were separated from the main house for many reasons. First and foremost was the chance of fire, and the other was that the heat generated would add too much warmth to the house during most of the year. Each kitchen had a large hearth for cooking. The bricks held their heat, which was also great for baking. As the fire died down and the hearth cooled, different foods were baked as some needed lower temperatures. Foods were not as varied as before the war; there were fewer supplies and much fewer people to feed. Each kitchen also had a large portable and sturdy wood table made to last and withstand the daily pounding from the cooks. It was often carried outside in warmer weather to evade the heat of the hearth.

Also, not far from the house were two pigeoneers. They were made of several cubby holes for pigeons surrounded by a cage-like sphere to keep them contained. Having pigeons was thought to be a symbol of status, and the birds were considered a delicacy at meals. Now there was just one active cage and about thirty pigeons left. They still were only eaten on special occasions such as birthdays and holidays.

Chapter 2

Next, the pair walked to the stables where Emanuel would have two horses saddled for the rest of the inspection. Emanuel was one of the eighteen slaves that elected to stay when all the other four hundred slaves left. They were all free to go as there was no one to stop them. These eighteen stayed with the promise of maintaining a place to live and food to eat in exchange for their work. The most important reason the three young couples stayed was to protect their children, which numbered seven among them. As their ages ranged from three to twelve years, they were too young to make the long trek north. Besides, the Johnsons had been good to them. They did not beat their slaves like many plantation owners, and Mr. Johnson had agreed to let any slave that had worked ten years receive their freedom papers. If a slave stayed after the ten years, they were paid for their work. It was not a lot of money as shelter and food were still provided. Many stayed after the ten years as they had loved ones at the plantation. These pleasantries temporarily ended with the death of Marie, Bella's cousin.

Slaves Emanuel and Kai had two children, ages three and ten. Roman and Sally also had two, ages five and eight years. Last of the young couples were Marcus and Georgia. They had three children, ages two, six, and twelve years. Noah, the ten-year-old, and Daniel, the twelve-year-old, also worked around the plantation. They were sweet boys, and Bella enjoyed talking to them. She tried to teach them proper grammar, but sometimes, she found herself forgetting grammar herself. The younger children always stayed close to their parents as they worked in the fields, the greenhouses, or anywhere else they happened to be. Most young slave children had run naked until about the age of ten as most owners would not provide any clothing for the growing little people. The Johnson were different; the clothing would be inexpensive, but denim pants and cotton shirts were provided twice each year for the men and simple dresses for the women. Fabric was given so the slave women could make clothes for their children. The females would tie their hair up in colorful cloth similar to how it had been done in Africa by their ancestors. The men would sometimes tie a piece of cloth around their head at the forehead to keep sweat out of their eyes. These slaves were overseen by Big George, and although he looked scary, he would never have harmed any of the rest of them, only protect them.

To complete the group of slaves were the domestic help. Raymond was in his fifties, an average-sized Negro man with a balding head and a big smile and two missing teeth. He worked around the house and helped keep the gardens tidy for Bella's mother. His wife was Emma. She was also in her fifties, short and overweight. Her silver-gray hair was always pulled back in a bun. Emma had soft brown eyes, and she gave the best hugs. She was an excellent cook and could make any food taste delicious, even beets.

Next was Ellie, a tall and slender woman with loosely curled black hair, which she always kept tied with a multicolored piece of cloth. Her skin was not as dark as the others. Emma told her it was because there was some white blood in her history. As she did not remember her parents, Ellie was not sure when that happened. It was not uncommon for plantation owners and their sons to take a slave to bed. These children were never recognized, but it had the effect of lightening the skin color. This "bedding" had also happened to Ellie as she was a beautiful woman, so now she had a daughter named Mimi. Like her mother, Mimi, had brown skin, not blackish, and was fifteen years. Instead of curly hair, it was more wavy, and she wore it long in a braid. Together, Ellie and Mimi kept the house clean, did the laundry, and helped wherever needed when they were not busy. Prior to the war, all slaves had to keep their own clothes clean, taking them to the stream for washing. They then built fires to help them dry. Now Ellie and Mimi did everyone's laundry. At this time of year, a large fire was built near where the laundry hung to dry as the temperatures were often in the high thirties to low fifties. Slaves did not always know exactly how old they were as they did not always live with their parents, and there may not be anyone to help them keep track.

Bella rode Sugar, a light-tan-colored quarter horse with a mahogany-colored mane, tail, and a white star on her forehead. Big George usually rode Tucker, a dark-walnut-colored quarter horse with a black mane and tail. These were two of three riding horses still on the plantation. The third, Fancy, was still young and could be a little skittish with noises. She was a chestnut-brown quarter horse with a black mane and tail.

"Good morning, Emanuel. How are Noah and his little brother?" Bella said as she approached the stables.

Emanuel responded, "Mor'n, Ms. Bella. They doing good."

Bella then said, "I would like to take Fancy out tomorrow. The more she is ridden, the calmer she will get."

"Yes, Ms. Bella. Sugar do need rid'n." Emanuel replied as he nodded.

"Thank you, Emanuel. You have a blessed day," Bella said as Emanuel tipped his hat and gave her a leg up and then handed her the reins.

The last remaining workhorses were two beautifully matched pairs. Dakota and Sadie were Shire Draft horses from England, gifts from Mary's parents when she married Jonathan. Their coats were a velvety black with coal-black manes and tails. This breed of horse was the largest and strongest of all workhorses. Young Daniel, although only twelve years, stood five feet tall. He was responsible for braiding and pinning up the workhorses' tails. He also groomed them, which he greatly enjoyed and was very proficient at doing. Dakota stood about seventeen hands and Sadie about fifteen hands. Hands were measured by marking the distance from the withers of a horse. The withers are the spinal processes in a horse's spine that join the neck to the rest of the horse's body. They are seen by people as a lump in their shoulder area. Since the withers are secure in place, they are used to measure horse height. Hands are measured from the top of the withers to the ground and equate to about four inches per hand. The other pair were Irish Draft horses standing about fifteen and thirteen hands tall. Blaze and Daisy were speckled gray with black around their feet and dark gray manes and tails. Although they were meant for breeding and pulling large carriages as needed, they were now used for plowing and moving the wagons. Each pair had given birth once in the past two years. When the colts were old enough, they were sold. Horses, especially workhorses, were in great demand.

After mounting, Bella and Big George rode toward the barn. The fields wouldn't be plowed for another six weeks. They still planted six small fields to raise their own corn, wheat, alfalfa, and indigo. Most of these crops were used for livestock or sold to neighbors. Indigo was the common source of blue dye for cotton material like denim. This could still be sold at a good price. Fortunately, Roman was a skilled "indigo slave." He had been trained to convert the plant into dye. All the other fields just sat empty; they had been used primarily for cotton. The plantation had also grown tobacco, rice, and potatoes in addition to the ones they grew now just in larger quantities. Now they grew smaller amounts in their vegetable garden.

Their small herd of cattle still numbered twenty-five plus five dairy cows. As Bella looked over at them she said, "Are any of the cows with calf?"

Big George said, "Yes, t'ree be com'ng soon."

Bella nodded and thought about the fact that each time a group of Confederate soldiers came through, a cow and a few chickens were butchered for them to eat. The meat along with several baskets of produce were part of the stash given. If it was a regiment, some of the tobacco still in the tobacco barn would also be given. Bella wanted to believe they were doing it to help, but she wasn't sure that now, two years in, the food wouldn't be taken whether they wanted to give it or not. This always made her think of her father and brothers. Were they eating enough? Were they in good health? Were they unharmed?

As they continued riding, Big George said, "There be th'rty chick'ns, eight'n sheep, nin' hogs, and tw'nty-five goats up front. We be littl' short on hay and straw. Should be good 'til next crop if keep 'em in the fields."

Bella nodded asking, "Baby chicks?"

Big George responded, "Put six an' rooster in th' oth'r coop an' ther' be tw'lve eggs they be sittn'g on. Check th'm each day."

Bella added, "Great, any other baby animals arriving soon?"

"T'ree of sheep, one hog, and nin' of goats. 'Member hog has many at a time" replied Big George.

Breeding their animals was keeping them in meat for themselves and for the soldiers that came through.

Then Bella noticed that of the five Moorish water cisterns, two were running low. This was surprising as there had been multiple rains and some snows during December. Hopefully, water wouldn't be an issue this summer. Then as they rode toward the greenhouses, the cloudy sky started to give way to some sunshine, a welcome sight. The greenhouses, like the livestock, were a saving grace now that the money was getting scarce.

Chapter 3

There were a total of five greenhouses, of which three were still active. They were located west of the main grounds, and they were still able to raise asparagus, pole beans, cabbage, broccoli, carrots, celery, okra, parsnip, rhubarb, spinach, tomatoes, and peas. Sometimes they would switch out to grow snap peas, beets, cauliflower, cucumbers, eggplant, lettuce, peppers, radishes, squash, turnips, and oyster plants. Oyster plants taste slightly like oysters but mostly like artichoke and are used like parsnips and carrots in soups and stews.

At least half or more of one side of one of the greenhouses was only used for herbs. Although herbs were used for fragrance and flavor, they were especially helpful for healing. Emma knew just which herbs to use for what. There was garlic to help with scurvy, deter fleas, and to use as an antibiotic. She would use sage to soothe a cough or sore throat. Sometimes—actually all the time—she mixed the herb in tea or milk to hide the taste. Thyme was used as an antiseptic. Marcus often made use of the garlic and thyme as he was always scraping a knee or elbow. Rue was used in the greenhouse to attract butterflies and other pollinators to the garden as well as parasitic wasps, (wasps that lay eggs on other harmful insects). So in the warmer months, the greenhouse doors may be left open for the pollinators, and so it won't get too hot inside. Mother and Bella especially liked that mint was planted as it made great hot tea. Emma, on the other hand, especially liked the parsley and oregano as they added a nice flavor to many of her dishes.

Several of the plants were ready for harvesting in two of the greenhouses and would keep two to three of the slaves busy today.

When Bella saw the slave women, she said, "Hello, ladies. How are you all doing today?"

All three women, Kai, Sally, and Georgia, said in unison, "Good, Ms. Bella."

"Big George tells me you ladies will be busy today harvesting lots of vegetables," Bella said as she dismounted to give each of the women a hug. Bella loved them for their kindness and honesty.

As she was hugged, Kai said, "Yes, Ms. Bella."

Then it was Sally's turn to be hugged. "We start work'n th'm some today."

Georgia finished with, "We do rest of work 'morrow and maybe some next day" as she received her hug.

Bella waved goodbye after she remounted her horse to continue the inspection.

Tomorrow, they would work on cleaning, canning, and storing the produce from today. Food storage could be found in the active kitchen, the inactive kitchen, the food prep room in the main house, and the cold storage shed. This shed was a cave-like hole dug into the side of a small mound just behind the kitchen. It had wood sides and wood pallets as a floor. Due to the front wall and door, this shed stayed very cool. The ground provided great protection from the heat of the sun. During the last year, the meals focused more around vegetables with a little meat than the other way around. They were currently using the smoked pork cured in the smokehouse about four days per week. The other days were rabbits or squirrels and sometimes a deer. In another month, work would need to be done in the fruit tree orchards. There were apple, peach, lemon, and cherry orchards.

Chapter 4

Hunting was the next activity for Bella as soon as breakfast was finished. The morning inspection with Big George took Bella about one to one and half hours. Upon her return, she would enter the house to the happy, yelling voices of her younger siblings. This was usually near 8:00 a.m. Mother usually did not come down until closer to 8:30 a.m. It never stopped amazing Bella that each time her mother descended the staircase, it was as if she floated like a feather. Her grace was always present even in the worst of times. Bella had not mastered her mother's grace and wasn't sure she ever would.

Annabella Marie was born March 17, 1845. She was tall at 5'7" and slender at just over 130 pounds. Her strawberry blonde hair was long and smooth. Bella's blond hair looked golden, but when the sunlight shone just right, there was the glow of strawberry tint. She liked to wear it down, but during the last year, she often pulled it back in a ponytail. She brushed it every day for fifty strokes; her mother insisted it was necessary. Bella had hazel eyes, the only one in her family, a mixture of her father's brown and mother's pale blue ones. When people looked at her, which color they saw depended on which color she wore. This made her feel special, and it was one of the few physical attributes she felt she had. Most of her education had been with tutors. Mother had wanted to send her to a finishing school like she had done, but they were located up in the New England states, and Mother was not comfortable with her being that far away.

ANNABELLA'S STORY

Her younger sister, Mary Margaret, called Margaret to distinguish her from her mother, had just celebrated a birthday, born January 25, 1848. She was now fifteen years and restless due to having only a few friends or things to do. She was petite like her mother but had light ash-brown hair. She liked to wear her hair long with side combs to keep it out of her dark-brown eyes. In the summer, her hair would turn lighter as she loved the outdoors. She usually wore a hat to shade her face and neck, but she did enjoy some time without it. Margaret would often read on the rear balcony or on one of the benches in the gardens around the house. Her favorite place was in the Japanese garden. Her books would be about places she wanted to explore: Europe, Africa, and China. She most wanted to go to Paris, France. Maybe after the war, her mother would take her. Margaret's only other joy came from playing the piano. Her mother had taught her, and she practiced every day. She could play for hours as it too could take her to faraway places and help her forget about their current conditions.

Bella's youngest sister, Elizabeth Joanna, called Lizzie by everyone except her mother, was not quite thirteen years. Born July 4, 1850, her birthday was also America's Independence Day. Prior to the war, it was such a special day, now there were mixed feelings about this day in the South. Like Bella, Lizzie had strawberry-blond hair, but she had more strawberry. She would have Ellie put a braid on either side of her face then pull them back into one letting about four inches of her hair hang loose. Their Grandmother Morgan had light-red hair so the girls were blessed with it whether they liked it or not. Lizzie was a petite little girl, and she would sing everywhere she went. At meals, on walks, during bath time, watching Emma prepare meals, everywhere. Fortunately for all those around her, she was very talented. Some of her songs she learned from her mother, some from Ellie and the other slave women, and some she just made up. The self-composed ones were always the sweetest and the funniest.

The youngest of the Johnson children was Marcus Allen, born October 10, 1855. He was just over five years when the war started. He looked just like his father and wore his hair short. Without a man in his life the last few years, he had become very mischievous.

He often followed both Raymond and Big George around when he could get away from his mother. He was not a bad child, but he did not like being surrounded by all the "girls" in the house.

Breakfast was a simple affair, but Mother insisted they still eat in the dining room. It was served as soon as Mother had spoken to her children to greet the day.

Mary said, "Good morning, my darlings."

Each child responded in kind, "Good morning, Mother."

As Ellie approached with some food, Mother said, "What delicious dish are we having today?"

Ellie replied, "Th' day we hav' corn bread and sausages, Ms. Mary."

"Thank you, my dear. Please go ahead with the serving," said Mother.

On other days it could be hot cakes with sausages or an omelet and fried potatoes. Some days it was just cold bread and a nice hash. In the past, all these tasty foods would have been available at once and served for breakfast.

Mother always wore one of her morning/day dresses. These dresses were beautiful but much simpler than her evening dresses/gowns. Day-wear dresses were high-necked as it was unseemly for a woman to show skin before late afternoon. Pale skin was the style, so necks and shoulders had to be covered to avoid the sun. Outdoors, during the day, women carried parasols or wore bonnets or hats to avoid sunlight. Mother looked best in blues and purples but occasionally wore a pale yellow or green day dress. They had fewer bows, ribbons, and buttons and would be a little shorter than evening attire, so movement was easier. Day dresses were seldom worn with hoops, just petticoats. Today was her favorite pale-emerald-green dress. She also had a piece of her hair jewelry on. It was a brooch with her husband's hair in it. Hair jewelry was a special way to remember loved ones separated by distance or death. A few hairs of the person were included in rings, brooches, bracelets, necklaces, earrings, or even watch chains. Mother had a piece of hair jewelry for her husband and each of her sons.

ANNABELLA'S STORY

Although her father was not especially pleased about the situation, Bella's oldest brother, Jonathan Jr., had taught her how to trap and shoot. While he would be home from the Virginia Military Academy, Jonathan would take Bella out into the woods. They started when Bella was ten years, and they focused on traps for rabbits and squirrels. Bella had no trouble trapping the animals, but it took her a few years before she could skin and clean them for eating. Now she was so thankful she had learned this skill. She and Raymond would do the hunting each morning. Sometimes they caught one or two critters and other days none. Once Bella turned fifteen years, Jonathan taught her to shoot a musket. Her aim had improved, but the first time she shot a deer, she wept. It had been a doe and such a delicate-looking animal. Jonathan had insisted she watch him and Raymond butcher the deer. But she could not make herself eat any of that meat. Now she fought down her anxiety of killing such timid animals as the family and slaves needed to eat. She shot one about every five to six weeks and a turkey or pheasant about once every three to four weeks. Now, Raymond and one of the other slaves would do the butchering, and Bella was very thankful they did.

Chapter 5

Bella's attire was not like it had been before the war. Ellie had taken a few of her day dresses and converted them into something resembling a wide pair of pants. When she was standing, she appeared to be in a dress, which kept her mother happy, but this style gave her the ability to more easily ride a horse and go hunting. Elllie and Mimi were both talented seamstresses. They had been able to modify not only her dresses but could turn old, unused clothes and outgrown attire into wearable clothes for the growing younger three. These clothes may not have been as fancy as they had before, but they did fit their maturing bodies. Marcus was the most difficult to sew alternative clothes for. There weren't as many material options for a young lad. Shoes were the hardest as they could only find a few of the older brothers' previous pairs still in good enough shape to use. Today she wore a dark-green outfit with a pair of her brother's old boots and one of his hunting jackets. The air was still chilly, so she donned a pair of her brother's old gloves and a dark scarf. Dark attire was important when hunting in the woods as was walking slowly and quietly. Raymond had helped Bella perfect her hunting skills. Today, they would check some of the traps along the creek. They walked in silence, but it was a happy quiet. It gave Bella time to just enjoy the scenery and remember.

Bella's mind drifted to an event that had happened last autumn. Marcus was using his free time to look at the birds. He thought he spotted a rare bird, the red-cockaded woodpecker. It was a small woodpecker with black-and-white laddered stripes on its wings.

They had white bellies, black heads, and white cheeks. They used their stiff tail feathers to balance them on the side of pines to peck at insects. Marcus saw the bird he thought was a red-cockaded woodpecker pecking at one of the pine trees in the front. As he approached the tree, the bird flew off. Marcus chased it and was so excited he followed it straight into the woods. He lost sight of it but kept walking deeper into the woods looking for it. Finally he realized he was lost. Marcus knew this was not good as he was only six going on seven years, and he wasn't allowed in the woods alone. He thought he was going back the way he came in, but then he stopped. Marcus sat down next to a tall tree and tried not to cry. What would happen to him? Would he be eaten by a wild pig, a panther, or that big, scary monster people say lived in the woods? The more he thought about the possibilities, the more scared he got, and tears ran down his face. Marcus decided he would stay just where he was and wait for someone to find him. Soon, he fell asleep on the ground.

Three hours had passed since Marcus walked into the woods, and everyone had been looking for him for the last two hours. It was getting close to sunset, and Mother was frantic. She was crying while sitting on the front porch whimpering about how she should have been watching him closer. Lizzie sat beside her mother, holding her hand. Lizzie was not allowed to hunt for him anywhere except the house. Meanwhile, Emma made Mother cups of tea to try to keep her calm.

All the slaves except Emma were looking and calling for him. Big George decided to look in the woods. He knew Marcus liked birds, so maybe he had followed one there. Big George called his name several times and then listened for a response. After about twenty minutes, Big George was about to give up but tried one more time to call out his name. Then…he heard something. He called again as loud as he could. He heard it again, a small sound but definitely a child.

Big George yelled for Marcus to start yelling and dancing around. "Make noise, lit' one, keep yell'n."

Marcus stood up and yelled as loud as he could, "Big George, Big George, I am over here. Help me."

"I com'n, boy. Keep yell'n." George said as he walked in the direction of the noise and soon saw the little boy.

Marcus saw Big George a few moments later and started running toward him.

Big George yelled again, "Stop, boy. Snakes abo't." He knew there were several poison snakes in the area and feared Marcus might startle one.

Marcus stopped and waited. He was so happy and stood in place as again tears ran down his cheeks. Big George scooped him up, held him tight, and started walking back to the house.

Marcus was holding Big George around his thick neck so tight, Big George had to pat his hands to loosen up.

As Big George came into sight by the others, screams of joy erupted. Bella ran toward them and hugged both of them while Marcus was still in Big George's arms. Big George continued toward the house as Mother rounded the corner. Big George set the boy down and the pair ran like lightning together. When they met, Mother fell to her knees and caught her son. She hugged him so tight that Marcus had to start padding her shoulders because he couldn't breathe. Now Marcus understood what Big George meant by "holding too tight boy." Teatime that day was a celebration, and Marcus promised he would never go into the woods again even if it was for a red-cockaded woodpecker. Everyone laughed.

Chapter 6

The primary creek on the Johnson Plantation was about a forty-five-minute walk. The creek was wide but shallow in several places. This made it easy for the wild animals to drink. There were several large boulders nearby where they were headed, some of them embroiled in green moss. It would turn a brilliant shade of shamrock in the warm weather. In the shallow areas, there was a spattering of smaller stones, which made crossing not so wet. The traps they checked today were on the far side of the creek, so Raymond and Bella crossed in a shallow area. They had seven traps to check. Two had rabbits, one a squirrel, and four were empty. They reset the traps and headed back.

As Bella looked down at the rabbits, she said, "Those rabbits are a little on the thin side."

Raymond replied, "It still be winter, Ms. Bella."

Bella nodded, saying, "I suppose they will still be good for Emma's stew. She is a masterful cook."

"When we sk'n the fur till thick and soft to make good blankets," Raymond finished the conversation, and they continued walking toward the house.

As the pair walked back to the house, the wind picked up sending a chill over Bella's face and rustling the few leaves left in the trees. Soon spring would be here, and everything would turn green and fresh again. This had Bella smiling. She loved springtime and watching all the buds grow and open creating an immense array of color.

This is how Bella spent most of her mornings, inspecting and hunting. She always used Sunday as a day of rest like the Lord had directed—after the inspection with Big George of course. Slaves would only do the minimal amount of chores like feeding the livestock on Sundays also. Mother and Father often read to them from the Bible talking to them about how to live as moral and good people, and now she used it as a source of comfort. Bella read a few pages each night and prayed for all the people suffering at this time; she knew that was a lot. Then each morning before she rose from her comfortable bed, Bella would thank the Lord for a peaceful night's sleep and the hopes that this day would be a fulfilling day and would be the end of the war. The fulfilling days would arrive, but she was still waiting for the end of the war.

Chapter 7

Bella removed all her outerwear and boots, washed her hands, and moved into the dining room for their midday meal. She usually also needed to go upstairs, wash her face, change clothes, and brush out her hair. Unlike breakfast, this meal was the main meal of the day. They would usually partake of this meal around 1:00 p.m. The three youngest had spent the morning with Mother and their lessons. The menu would consist of soup or stew, roast or boiled meat, calves' head, turkey, chicken, fish, or ham. The wild game was usually put into the stew. There would always be several vegetables and pudding or stewed fruit and, on special occasions, pie.

The dining table would be set with a dinner plate and soup bowl in the center. Dinner fork to the left of the plate and napkin just left of that. Dinner knife just right of the plate with the sharp edge pointing toward the plate and a soup spoon to the right of it. A butter plate with a butter knife laid diagonally across it and was just above the fork on the left. There was a water glass placed above the knife and spoon on the right. Wine glasses had not been on the table since Uncle Edwin had died. If dessert was served, the plate and appropriate utensil was brought out at that time. This along with the cup and saucer for coffee or tea also came out after they ate.

One of those special occasions happened last summer, before Marcus got lost in the woods. Lizzie, everyone's favorite singer, went dancing and singing just in front of the house. It was midmorning on a Saturday, and she decided she wanted to see the fish in the pond at the Japanese garden. Great-Uncle Edwin liked unusual things. He heard about a fish called koi and how they would look good in a Japanese garden. Koi were reportedly good for eating and added color to a pond. He ordered some and stocked his and Father's ponds. Each built a special pond according to plans Edwin was given. The pond needed both shallow and deep areas so the fish could swim in the best temperature for them depending on the time of the year.

These fish were beautifully colored, lots of orange, white, and black. Lizzie had liked these fish and thought they needed a song. She would watch them and make one for them to hear. The pond was very shallow close to the house. This first layer was covered in stones and gradually deepened for a distance of about four feet and to a depth of about three feet, then a drop off of three feet. This step down continued until there was a five-foot square area nine feet down at the bottom. As it was not hot but cool, the fish were easy to see especially if you threw them some food.

Lizzie had just turned eleven years, and her songs were getting better. As she approached the pond, she could see some of the fish in the area just beyond the shallow part. She started humming and wanted a closer look. She took off her shoes and stockings and pulled her dress up so it wouldn't get wet. The fish darted away when she stepped into the water. So Lizzie took a few small steps deeper and stopped. The fish returned and swam closer. Now she stepped closer to the edge then one more step, and she could feel the edge of the first step down with her toes. The water was below her waist, so only her petticoat was getting wet. She leaned over and leaned a little more and…splash. Lizzie had fallen in, and she panicked. She started splashing and yelling, splashing and yelling. Although the depth was only five feet, all her kicking and splashing had moved her into the next area, which was over her head.

ANNABELLA'S STORY

Slave Marcus had just finished unloading some produce from a wagon he had picked up from one of the greenhouses into one of the kitchens for cleaning and preparing. He was walking back to the wagon when he thought he heard a noise. He walked a few more steps toward the noise and heard yelling and then saw Lizzie. Slave Marcus took off. He was a very fast runner, lean and fit. He also started yelling, "In ta pond, in ta pond." Others heard, and Bella had been one of them. She rushed out to see what was going on. Bella saw Slave Marcus running to the pond so she did also. When Marcus arrived, Lizzie was still splashing and yelling, but she was sinking for longer periods of time. Slave Marcus could not swim, but he knew Lizzie was in trouble, so he walked out to the edge of the shallow area. He squatted down and reached for her, but Lizzie was just out of reach. She looked so scared. Marcus jumped in and then realized he could stand. He reached for Lizzie again, and she was pawing at him in a huge panic. He held her tight and talked to her, saying she would be fine; she was safe. Bella reached the pond next and walked out to take Lizzie from Marcus. Just about then, Big George arrived and helped pull Marcus out of the water.

Lizzie was soaked but started to calm down. Bella gave her to Georgia and asked her to be taken to the house. There she knew Mother and Emma would take excellent care of Lizzie. Meanwhile Bella turned, walked over to Slave Marcus, and gave him the biggest hug she could, saying "Thank you." She got even wetter, but she didn't care; her sister was safe. Then she kissed his cheek and started for the house herself. Marcus had never been kissed by a white woman even if it was just on the cheek. He rubbed where she kissed and started walking back, taking his shirt off as he went. He too would need dry clothes.

Chapter 8

After their meal, it was Bella's turn to be the teacher. Although their Mother was intelligent, numbers were not her specialty. Bella had taken to working with numbers with ease, so she would spend a minimum of one but no more than two hours with the children on their math skills. Margaret could do simple equations for adding and subtraction, but this was definitely not a subject she enjoyed. Bella tried to explain she used math every time she played the piano to keep beat. However, Margaret did not see it that way. Lizzie and Marcus, however, came to it naturally. Lizzie used her skills in helping Bella with the ledgers on the livestock and food supplies. She also counted the stored food stocks weekly with Mimi's assistance.

Marcus would need these skills as he grew older, but for now, he counted the birds in the trees and how many of each kind. He used reference books he found in their library to identify the various birds. He knew the ones that came from the north during the colder months. This included morning doves, robins, cardinals, eastern bluebirds, and blue jays. Marcus would listen to hear the woodpeckers. Two of his favorites were the downy woodpecker and the red-bellied woodpecker. The downy woodpeckers were white and black with black-and-white speckled wings. The male had an orange spot on his head, while the females did not. Marcus was talking to Bella when he said, "I still don't understand why the red-bellied woodpeckers are called that."

Bella replied, "To me they look like the ones you call a downy woodpecker."

Marcus nodded, saying, "Yes, they do look like the downy woodpecker, but the boys have red from the beak back along the head to their back. And the girl ones have less red on their head. But neither have any on their belly."

Bella just laughed.

Sometimes, Marcus would name the birds if he thought he saw the same bird three or four times. He was also proficient at identifying the Carolina wren, the house sparrow, and the Carolina chickadee. He wanted to know why some were called Carolina birds; they were in Mississippi. The most impressive thing to Bella and her mother was that he could tell the difference between a house finch and a purple finch.

Marcus put up his hand. "Listen…do you hear that?"

Mother replied, "What?"

"The short low call, it's like a warbling sound," said Marcus.

Mother looked at him, saying, "Which bird is that?"

Marcus smiled and said with pride, "The purple finch. He is fatter, has a reddish color and a smaller tail. The house finch is noisier and chirpier."

"Did you mean *more chirpy*?" Mother responded in her corrective voice.

Marcus's shoulders sagged a little as he said, "*More* chirpy not chirpier. Mother, I will try to remember."

Chapter 9

The next few hours of the day before the evening meal or teatime were spent how each person desired. Mother and Margaret may play the piano. Lizzie may walk or sit somewhere to sing. Marcus would roam the yards looking for birds. He had started learning about the different kinds of trees and different kinds of insects. Bella, she would go to her room to relax. Sometimes she may take a short nap, read, or write letters to her father and brothers. At first, Bella would send the letters, but after the first year of the war, she just kept them in a box to hopefully give to each of them later.

Other days, Bella would go horseback riding through the empty fields and woods. She loved to ride. Galloping on Sugar gave her the feeling of being free and alive. One afternoon, she decided to ride over to the house Uncle Edwin and Marie had lived in. On their ride over, Bella wanted to work Sugar on her various gaits: walk, trot, canter, and gallop. They started at a walk, and she could smell the fresh air, the lilacs in bloom, and the bees flying near her. Next, they went up to a trot. Bella had to keep her in check so she would stay at that pace. Once she had it under control, they moved up to a canter. By this time, they were approaching the property. The pair kept this pace until they reached the first open field. Off they went at a full gallop. Bella thought Sugar enjoyed this speed as much as she did. Bella slowed them down, turned, and headed back to the empty house.

She dismounted and led Sugar at a walk to cool her down. The closer she got to the house, she realized something didn't look right.

ANNABELLA'S STORY

Then it hit her: The back door was ajar and a window was broken. Four slaves lived in one of the cabins to keep the property tidy. Bella saw one of them working nearby and motioned him over. She talked to him about the window and door, and he explained that he had not noticed. Bella tied Sugar to a post, and together they went inside. There did not appear to be any damage, but they found two confederate soldiers looking raggedly and sleeping on two of the beds. Their presents awoke the soldiers, and they were startled at being caught.

Bella said, "What are you doing here? Where is your unit?"

The two soldiers jumped off the beds and pulled out knives.

Bella and the slave took a step back. "We have no weapons. We will not hurt you."

The first soldier spoke, "We don't want to fight no more. All our friends are dying."

The second soldier then said, "Just let us go. We can leave now."

Bella hesitated but said, "Are you hurt? Hungry?"

The second soldier spoke again, "No, not hurt, but yes, hungry. Can you help us?"

"I will give you food, but are you saying you are deserters?" Bella asked with some disgust in her voice.

The first soldier who appeared very young spoke as his eyes welled up. "We just can't fight anymore. There is so much blood and bodies in pieces, some of the pieces missing even. Just can't anymore." The second soldier patted his shoulder as he spoke.

Bella finished the conversation with "You need to come with me then be on your way. I will not tell anyone I saw you, but you cannot stay here."

The two men rose and followed Bella out of the house. She asked the slave who entered with her to walk them down to the main grounds of the plantation. Then she continued to walk around the house and then the grounds immediately near the house. She mounted Sugar and rode the rest of the property with buildings. Bella made a mental note of some items needing work, including the broken window. The two, Bella and Sugar, returned in the same manner they arrived, working from a walk to a gallop. Upon returning to the stables, she asked Daniel to walk Sugar for a little while so she could cool down.

Bella went to the house and found the two soldiers. They had been fed. Bella asked Emma to give them some food, then she looked at the men. "I understand why you are doing this, but I do not condone it. *Don't* ever come back here again. Next time, I will shoot you both."

Chapter 10

Ellie and Mimi would clean the rooms and do the laundry during the mornings. Then they would either help Emma in the kitchen or go work with some of the other slaves on that day's tasks. All the slaves usually worked from about 7:00 a.m. until about 7:00 p.m. during the planting or harvesting days but about 8:00 a.m. to 5:00 p.m. during other days. All the remaining eighteen slaves had moved into the second floors of the two kitchens. In the warmer months, more would sleep in the inactive kitchen, and during the colder months, especially the women and the children, in the active kitchen. Some of the items from the cabins were moved into these areas to provide as much comfort as possible. The kitchens were not only closer to the house but were built much better as most of the slave cabins were wood boards and not well insulated. There were windows on the second floor that could be closed with wooden shutters. The beds just had straw mattresses, but it was better than the floor. Every other year, six mattresses would be restuffed or completely remade. This was done last year.

The family would dress up slightly for the evening activities and meal. The meal was known as teatime. Mother would be the fanciest dressed as she was the same size as she ever was. This meal was somewhere between breakfast and dinner for quantity and items served. There could be cold or hot bread, corn bread, or milk toast, stewed fruit, and sometimes frizzled beef. Tea time took place about 7:00 p.m. in one of the parlors. Which parlor would depend on the time of the year and the temperatures outside.

Conversations during teatime were very casual. Everyone would talk about what they did, saw, or read that day. Bella never broached the subjects of finances, status of the plantation, or any other topics usually discussed and decided by the men of the family.

When Uncle Edwin was still in charge of the plantation, Bella herself knew little about its workings. However, during his last six months, he shared as much as he could. Light conversation would continue, and then at about 9:00 to 9:30 p.m., everyone would retire for the day. Usually, Marcus went a little earlier, but he didn't like to.

Most conversations went like this:

Mother usually started by saying, "My dear Margaret, what did you do with your afternoon?"

Margaret replied with great enthusiasm, "I finished a book on Greece. This country is surrounded by water made up of four different seas. There are three thousand islands and many mountains."

Marcus chimed in, "I would like to climb a mountain. Can I go?"

Mother quickly responded, "Maybe someday, Marcus, but not until your father returns."

Then it was Lizzie's turn, "I made a new song today. Would everyone like to hear it?"

"Of course, we would love to," said Mother.

Lizzie started singing. "I had a little turtle—his name was Tiny Tim. I put him in the bathtub to see if he could swim. He drank up all the water and ate a bar of soap. And now he's in his bed with bubbles in his throat. Bubble, bubble, bubble, bubble, bubble, bubble, bubble, bubble, bubble, bubble, *pop!* Lizzie jumps up when she says pop, and everyone laughs.

While Bella was laughing, she said, "That was wonderful, you silly girl."

"I counted five blue jays in the big tree in the front. And did you know that big tree is called a red maple? And I watched Raymond skin the rabbits caught from this morning. I really watched just before dinner. Sorry, Mother, you weren't watching me," Marcus said without taking a breath.

ANNABELLA'S STORY

Marcus tended to talk fast and get all his thoughts in before anyone could interrupt him.

Mother gave him one of her looks for a few seconds and then smiled. There would be a few more exchanges and then off to bed.

Mother would assist Marcus then Lizzie in preparing for bed. Ellie and Mimi would assist Margaret, Bella, and Mother as it was needed. Raymond always ensured that all the windows and doors were locked and secured. This had not been a worry until about one year ago, and most of the slaves had run off. Raymond would feed the three dogs currently on the property shortly before dark. He would leave them loose to help protect or at least make everyone aware if intruders or wild animals approached. Their three dogs were two large bloodhounds named Bacon and Ginger and one mastiff named Bandit. They were very protective of the family and livestock on the plantation. However, they were trained to attack if needed, so everyone needed to use caution when approaching. Some plantation owners used *Dogo Cubano*, otherwise known as Cuban bloodhound or Cuban bullmastiff. These dogs were vicious and used to scare slaves and chase them down if they escaped. Sometimes they were allowed to bite the escapee to teach that slave and the other slaves what could happen. These owners, however, did not want the slave dead as then they lost money and a strong worker. Raymond had always been responsible for the Johnson dogs' care, so they were very good with him. Bella kept one loaded musket in her bedroom and one by both the front and back doors. These muskets were

Bloodhounds above Mastiff below

moved each morning, so no one, especially Marcus, would accidentally shoot themselves. Raymond and Big George also kept muskets but both were better with knives. The other slave men would fight if needed, but to date, there was only one time there was an issue.

One night shortly after Marcus had gotten lost, the dogs started barking. Raymond, Big George, and Bella all jumped out of bed with a start. The dogs continued to bark and run toward the inactive kitchen. All three people grabbed a gun and ran out in their night clothes. They headed to the kitchen where the dogs were and heard the sound of men yelling. Inside they found four slaves, three of which were getting bitten by one of each of the dogs. Big George called the dogs off; the three that had been bitten fell to the floor crying out in pain. The fourth was up on the worktable. The men had arrived before Bella as they were just on the next kitchen's second floor. When Bella appeared, she wanted to know what was going on.

The slave on the table said, "We's jus' try'n to get food. We be run'n north."

Everyone looked at Bella. She responded, "I understand. We will not harm you anymore. I am sorry the dogs bit you, but you are trespassing." Bella pointed at Raymond. "Please get Emma to look at their injuries and fix them up. Big George, please help get this one on the table." She pointed at the one that seemed the worst as he was bitten by Bandit. "I will go in and get the last bit of food from today and bring it out. Raymond, after you get Emma, please get some water to clean them up and for them to drink."

Bella left feeling both upset and mad. She didn't really care that the slaves were running, and she understood why they would run at night, but why go to another plantation to steal when it was likely they would be shot? At this rate, they were unlikely to make their destination. The rest of the family were in the prep kitchen to see what was going on. Bella explained and asked everyone to go back to bed. Mother agreed and shooed the younger children back to their rooms. Bella returned to the kitchen where the slaves were and saw everything was progressing along. Ellie, Mimi, and two of the other slave women were assisting. The third stayed with their children. Bella dropped off the food, saying, "After you all get them fixed up, take them upstairs where the other men are, so they can rest, and I will decide in the morning what to do."

The next morning, Bella found the four runaway slaves were not as bad off as originally thought. Both Big George and Raymond were in the inactive kitchen waiting for her.

Bella said, "You four may stay one more day, but stay out of sight. If anyone finds you here, I also will have trouble. I will give you no money but will send extra food with you." Bella left the building, and all the slave men looked at her as she left.

Raymond said, "She be mad at y'u. She a good lady—y'u stay hid'n, or me and Big George will take care of y'u 'rselves."

The four slaves stayed all day out of sight and left that night to continue their journey north. Emma told them how to tend to their wounds, and they were given food. They tried to get some of the other slaves to go with them, but they all refused and just wished them good luck.

Bella thought of that night, as recently there were the sounds of distant cannon fire. This caused her to be greatly concerned. What was coming?

Chapter 11

It was Sunday afternoon, and Bella was thinking of her sixteenth birthday. It had been one of the most wonderful days of her young life. It was the morning of March 17, 1861, and although the weather hadn't turned warm yet, the sunshine was bright, and the rays shone down like gifts from heaven. Her grandmother Morgan said they were the graces of God shining down on his beautiful creatures. She said that when she was a girl, she would put glass jars to capture the rays and thus the graces of God. Bella always thought that was so precious.

She couldn't sleep the night before her birthday as today would be a party to celebrate her officially becoming a young lady. In May would be the Debutante Ball. There, all the young ladies sixteen to eighteen years of age dressed in her finest and were introduced to society. Their dresses would be strictly floor-length pure white ball gowns, and they also wore long white gloves and a decorative piece in their hair. This hairpiece might be similar to a tiara with different-colored stones, a woven flowered piece, or a jeweled hair comb. Then they were eligible to be seen by the local young men of the area. At the Debutante Ball, the young men wore white ties and tails. Everyone else looked their best in either colorful and elaborate ball gowns or in black tails. Sometimes the gentlemen were older and still looking for a suitable wife or the first wife had died. "Being seen" meant the men could call on you at your home between the hours of 3:00 to 5:00 p.m. with a guardian or chaperone present. Some would bring flowers, candy, or both, but they always brought a big smile and the prospects of a well-to-do future.

ANNABELLA'S STORY

Today, the party would be close family and friends of her parents, including a few dignitaries from the area. Mother had a special dress designed for Bella just for this occasion, and it would take a few hours to get ready for the event. It was a rich shade of royal blue made of crepe satin fabric. This color would have her hazel eyes sparkling more blue than green or brown. Satin had been around for several centuries in England and China. Then the crepe fabric was developed as a need for a rugged and pebbly fabric came into existence. Fashion experts were looking for something lustrous but stiff. Then some man thought that both fabrics' best should be combined. Hence a reversible fabric was manufactured, which had a glossy satin fabric on one side and a rugged textured crepe on the other. This combined fabric was smooth and soft, had an excellent drape flowing like water waves, was shiny on one side and pebbly on the other. When both sides were used in various parts of a dress, they provided an excellent contrast in a gown. The fabric was also very durable, so frequent swings around a dance floor were unlikely to give way to any tears in the gown.

Bella's gown had come from London and was altered upon arrival by a local seamstress. Unlike morning or day dresses, evening attire like Bella's gown, featured drop-shoulder sleeves, low necklines, and voluminous skirts held out by layers of petticoats. But today, it would be a hoop. Bella didn't really like hoops. They were horizontal circles of thin steel held in place by vertical strips of fabric. Bella thought they were uncomfortable while walking, sitting, or just moving at all. The bodice was somewhat lower than Bella's actual waistline and lined for support and closed in front with buttons.

Bodice and skirt fabrics were matched. The sleeves were known as bishop sleeves; gathered shoulder seam, widest at the elbow, and narrowed at the wrist. Bella's bishop sleeves were layered sleeves and the undersleeve would be showing. This undersleeve, called a negative sleeve, was sky blue and showed when the outer sleeve, royal blue, was caught up on the outer side of the elbow, leaving the royal blue portion of the sleeve at the back of the arm hanging. The hem of the skirt was bound by a strip of matching fabric. This fabric could be removed and replaced when the hem showed wear.

Bella's breakfast this morning consisted of corn bread, sausages, and an omelet with vegetables inside. The vegetables included onions, green peppers, and a little sage. She liked to grind black pepper over her omelet and butter on her corn bread. She had a small glass of milk and hot peppermint tea. Bella spent the morning on her studies, but it was difficult as she was distracted. Her tutor gave up, and she went for a walk through the gardens and the stables.

Dinner was a festive to-do, very formal. The dining table was covered with a thick baize under a pure white linen tablecloth. The baize reduced noise and made the table look handsome as without it, the table would look thin and not as elegant. The tablecloth was embroidered with violets and yellow pansies in each corner and an elaborate circle of the same in the center of the rectangle table. Inside the circle was a display of green winter pine foliage, along with the silver-gray foliage of the artemisia in a low ceramic beige vase. The center of the vase was loaded with dwarf blue and violet irises and white Shasta daisies all grown in one of the greenhouses especially for this occasion. Other flower arrangements were placed all about the foyer and the ballroom. The special china had been rewashed and the special silver utensils taken out and polished. There were gold chargers placed at each chair for those guests to be in attendance for the dinner. It would start at 2:00 p.m. The menu was planned two weeks in advance and would consist of the following:

> Course 1: Mutton broth with a few vegetables or roasted tomato bisque

Course 2: Fish including both bass and catfish with either
- garlic sauce—-garlic, butter, lemon juice, and parsley;
- fresh herb sauce—parsley, arugula, marjoram, oregano, vinegar, and garlic; or
- mint sauce—mint, garlic, vinegar, and sugar (for a sweeter taste).

Course 3: Roast veal, steaks, roast pig, and mutton with currant jelly; vegetables of boiled onions with cream sauce, spinach with hard-boiled egg slices, boiled potatoes, corn pudding, peas with butter, and stewed carrots

Course 4: Dessert: peach pie, plum pudding, custard with lemon or orange creams, and spice cake

The rest of the dining table had a fish fork and dinner fork to the left of the charger. There was a dinner knife, a fish knife, and a soup spoon to the right. This saved the trouble of replacing a knife and fork or spoon as each course was brought on. A napkin was neatly folded on the charger. A piece of each kind of bread, cut an inch thick and three inches long, would be placed on the bread plate just before the meal was to start. The breads for today would be corn bread, fruit bread, and Sally Lunn bread.

Water and red and white wineglasses were all placed on the table at each charger. The water glass was filled just before the dinner was announced. All the wine intended to be served were decanted and placed conveniently at different points on the table. Father would select the wines this morning to be served today. At opposite sides of the table were pepper mills, and each plate had a small bowl with a corresponding spoon known as a salt cellar, both for seasoning. The plates needed for the different courses were placed on the sideboard. A finger bowl was by each plate, half-filled with water with a slice of lemon. This left a pleasant odor on the fingers after pressing them in the bowl. The salt cellar and finger bowl were placed just above the charger between the bread plate and crystal glasses.

Later, dinner would be announced by the dining-room maid. A few extra young slave girls were brought in to help with the dinner. They were needed periodically, so extra clothes and training was provided for them so they would be ready when needed. A bell was never rung for a meal. Bells did very well for country inns and steamboats but not in private houses. The warm dishes, not *hot* dishes, would be kept in a tin closet until the moment of serving. A plate of each kind of bread would be on the sideboard along with soup tureens; the soups would be brought to the boiling point just before serving to keep it warm.

Chapter 12

It would take Bella at least two hours to be ready for the party. Thank goodness Ellie would help her. Southern women wore many layers of clothing. First, Bella would undress from her morning clothes, wash up, and then start over. She put on clean drawers, underpants made of soft cotton, trimmed in lace with a drawstring and ending just below her knees. Next would be the chemise, a long undershirt made of linen. Ellie would help her put on her stockings held up with garters. Bella's were thick black stockings due to the cool temperatures.

The second layer would be her corset stiffened with whalebone and laced at the back to accentuate a small waist. Bella liked the corset even less than the hoop. Ellie would tighten it until it was snug and stop. Now she would put on one petticoat and hoop. Then it was the sky-blue camisole, but sometimes, she wore a petticoat bodice or corset cover instead of a camisole.

The fourth layer was her new royal-blue bodice and skirt designed just for this day. The skirt was placed first as the bodice would cover the top of the skirt. It would look like one piece when complete. Like most women of the day, the Johnson women wore solid fabrics. Stripes and plaids were limited to the very wealthy as matching pieces of fabric used more material. Small prints like calico were easier to match and mend. Calico prints were usually dark to hide stains. Bella had several dresses in different calico prints as she liked variety. Ellie helped Bella with her black leather belt with the gold buckle and her new shiny black slippers made of satin and done in knit at the top. Last would be her new white shawl and long white gloves. She would only be wearing the gloves during the party as she could be a little messy while eating, and most ladies did not wear them to eat. Bella would be extra careful at this meal so as not to get any spills on her new clothes. One of the final touches was a white knit drawstring purse with one of the items inside being a white handkerchief with an embroidered *A* for *Annabella*. On other occasions, Bella may have worn her button-up boots especially when they were to be outside at an event during the summer. She didn't like bonnets or parasols, but she would wear a wide-brimmed hat. She had them in many colors to match her various outfits.

Ellie was excellent in doing up Bella's hair. Like other women of the South, Bella had pale skin and a rounded face. Her hair would be parted down the center and drawn back, with soft loops on each side of her face that would accentuate it. These loops would be puffed out with a "rat," a small net stuffed with hair gathered during brushing. To make her hair extra special, the side hair hung in loose ringlets from a central part. Her jewelry would be small-sized, rosy-gold delicate dangling earrings and one oval vertical brooch. Although it could be worn at the neckline at the top of the collar during the day, Bella's would be worn at the top of her lower-cut neckline on her ballgown. Matching chunky bracelets would be worn over her gloves on each wrist, and Bella would hold a fan, not because it would be humid but to hide her face when necessary. Her six-inch folding fan was painted with colorful and elaborate designs. Bella sometimes laughed when it was inappropriate, hence the fan. Fine ladies, according to Bella's mother, never painted their faces, so no color was added to her lips or cheeks. By the time Bella was ready, the dinner guests were already arriving at the plantation.

The meal would only be for her immediate family, her mother's parents, Grandmother and Grandfather Morgan, her father's Uncle Edwin, and his daughter, Marie. That would make twelve for dinner. Later, five more families would be joining for the party, which would feature music and dancing. Bella was so very blessed that her two older brothers would be home for her birthday and party. Father

ANNABELLA'S STORY

had requested they be allowed to leave their assignments, Jonathan from the US Army and Andrew from the Virginia Military Academy. Unbeknownst to Bella, but her father knew it would be the last time they would all be together for a long time. The rumors were true; war was coming.

Emma, as always, with the help of several other slaves, had put together a delicious meal. Bella was allowed to drink some red wine with her meal; it would take some getting used to. Several conversations were taking place all through dinner. As there were so many people, two or three would chat together, thus the several conversations. Bella was seated between her two big brothers.

Jonathan looked at his sister, saying, "Bella, you look beautiful today. Your dress really sets off your eyes."

Bella smiled then said, "Thank you, Jonathan. And you look very handsome in your uniform. Where did you say you were stationed?"

"I am in St. Louis, Missouri, inspecting various forts in the area," Jonathan responded.

Andrew gave his brother a look, saying, "Isn't that boring?"

Jonathan leaned in toward Andrew behind Bella's back, speaking quietly, "It would be if I didn't get to fight with some of the fort's men from time to time. Are you still thinking of going to West Point, or will you be doing *something* else?"

Andrew knowing he was talking about the potential for war and which side each of them would be on said, "Not now, Jonathan. Today is Bella's day."

Bella looked from one brother to the next. "What are you two whispering about?"

Jonathan winked at Bella. "We were deciding which of us was going to dance with you first."

They all three chuckled and moved on to how Andrew was doing at Virginia Military Academy.

A few hours later, the guests arrived for the party. Bella had five friends among the guests that were close to her age. They had a delightful time singing, dancing, and chatting like all teenage girls like to do. Bella danced with her father, Jonathan, and Andrew several times. She even danced with Marcus a couple of times. He wasn't very good yet but was definitely enthusiastic. She truly enjoyed watching her parents dance a few times; they looked so good together.

Chapter 13

Jonathan Samuel Johnson, Bella's father, known as John to family and friends, was a big man. He was 6'1" tall and just over 200 pounds. He was born May 5, 1815, in Vicksburg, Mississippi. John had mid-length dark-auburn hair and sweet pecan-colored eyes. His father, Samuel Alexander Johnson, had owned and started the plantation. It had passed to John upon his early death. His mother had died several years ago from typhoid fever. John had added another five-hundred-plus acres by purchasing two smaller plantations over the last eight years. These smaller farms were located close to the original plantation and had doubled the size of his family holdings. There were houses and buildings on each property, and they had been put to good use. John's in-laws were living in the bigger of the two houses, and John's uncle Edwin and his daughter were living in the other. Edwin and John worked together to become one of the biggest cotton producers in the area. Although Edwin was much older than John, he had suffered from malaria in his teens and wasn't as healthy as most people his age. Thus, John was responsible for the plantation and the finances of the family. Edwin was, however, very intelligent but tired easily, so he assisted John with the ledgers and in discussing future plans.

Edwin Thomas Johnson, born February 15, 1790, was seventy-one years when Bella celebrated her sixteenth birthday. He was not a large man, about 5'9" and 170 pounds. He, like his brother and nephew, had brown hair, but was balding, and dark eyes, though just a little lighter than John's. His daughter, Marie Charlotte, was born

August 8, 1820. Unfortunately, Marie's mother died that same day. Although everyone celebrated the birth, they were deeply saddened by the death. Marie had light-almond hair with a small patch of blond that was called a birthmark and gray-green eyes. She wore her hair down and always had some sort of barrette to style her hair to one side. She was sly and somewhat homely, but she was a wonderful older cousin to John's children. She loved to read all kinds of books and would read to the children when they were young. Marie liked to animate the book's characters with different voices and sometimes actions, which made the story more interesting and also funny. She never married but spent her time taking care of her father and managing the home.

Once, several years ago before Jonathan Junior was born, there was a man named Oliver Douglas who showed an interest in Marie. He came to Mississippi from Pennsylvania to sell a new form of cotton gin. Marie met him when he came to visit her father. They talked for a few minutes, and Marie was smitten. He was very handsome and flirted with Marie, which she was not accustomed to. A few days later, Marie just happened to be on the Johnson Plantation when Oliver came to see Samuel Johnson. Again, he flirted with her, and she felt both excited and embarrassed. The next day, Oliver called on Edwin to ask to see Marie. Edwin agreed, so Oliver came several times to visit Marie at her home. There was always a chaperone present, but the two grew to care for each other, or so she thought. After about a month, Oliver was to move on to another area. He wanted to take Marie with him so asked for her hand in marriage. Marie agreed, and arrangements were made between Edwin and Oliver on a dowry and when the wedding would take place. Oliver would get set up in his next town with the dowry money then return for the wedding. Marie and Oliver said their goodbyes, but the night before he left, he seduced her. From that day forward, Marie would never see Oliver again. When it became clear that Oliver was not coming back, Marie was devastated and would have nothing to do with any man again.

Jonathan Samuel Jr. was born November 15, 1840. At the age of twenty-one years, he was 6'2" and a solid 225 pounds. He was muscular and a very handsome young man. His hair was dark brown with just a hint of red and the most beautiful walnut-colored eyes. Jonathan started attending the Virginia Military Academy in the autumn just before he turned the age of fourteen. The Academy opened in 1839, providing both academic and military training. Since the cadets lived there, the bond among them grew very strong. Many of the graduates went on to West Point and a military career. Jonathan had attended the academy for five years before joining the US Army. He was very content and currently stationed in Missouri. He moved quickly through the ranks and was now a first lieutenant. Jonathan hoped to make captain soon. Other than his family, no one called him Jonathan. His friends called him John, and his fellow soldiers called him lieutenant. Bella loved him in his uniform; he would look menacing if he weren't family.

Andrew Mathew, the second son, was born on September 8, 1842. At the age of eighteen years, he was not as tall as his brother and father. He stood 5'10" and was just under 200 pounds. with a muscular body. He had copper-brown hair and ash-brown eyes. He too started attending the Virginia Military Academy at the age of fourteen years. Although not a bad student academically, Andrew excelled in his military studies. He had yet to decide his next step but thought he would go to West Point starting next year. He wore his VMA uniform home for Bella's birthday party. He too looked very handsome in his uniform.

They were to have a family picture taken before the brothers left. Both Father and Mother were very proud of their sons and the rest of their children. All the Johnson men wore their hair mid-length to a little long. If the length was longer, it was so that the hair could be tied back with a thin string of leather in a ponytail. Unlike many men of the time, they were all clean-shaven.

Chapter 14

Soon after Bella turned sixteen, the Civil War started. It was April 12, 1861. Father and Andrew both enlisted in the Confederate Army. Father had previous military experience and assumed the rank of major. Under his command was Andrew, where he was promoted to first lieutenant. Prior to Father's departure, he put Uncle Edwin in charge of everything. It was thought the war would be short and there would be two countries, the North and the South, or more precisely, the United States of America and the Confederate States of America. Grandmother and Grandfather Morgan had been through a war and had no desire to go through another. They were moving back to England for a while and encouraged Mother and all the remaining children to go with him. Mother refused as Father said it would not last long.

The first year of the war, the Johnson Plantation ran as it always had. Slaves plowed, planted, and harvested crops. The path outside the gate on the north side of the main grounds led to the schoolhouse on the right and then the laundry building. Continuing north led to the large barn used to store straw and hay for the livestock. This was also where the dairy cows were milked. Directly behind the barn were the cattle pastures with a separate pasture for the sheep and goats. To the west of the barn and pastures was a tobacco drying barn. The slave cabins were located both to the west and south of this barn. The overseer's house was near to the cabins but closer to the main grounds. Outside the west gate, used for wagons to deliver food to the kitchens was a large open field of grass and wildflowers. At the north end of the field was an in-ground cave-like building used for the cold storage of produce. At the south end of the field were the pigeon cages, and then a large grove of trees continued south to the main road.

East of the trees was another large field of grass and wildflowers. These types of fields were used when the plantation owner could not or did not want to use that area for crops and would reduce the amount of grass that needed to be attended to with an abundant flow of color. The drive from the house to the main road was lined with ginkgo and red maple trees. These trees provided excellent shade during the warmer months and unbelievable colors of burnt red and golden yellow in the autumn.

Outside the east gates, wide enough for carriages, stood most of the plantation buildings all in a long row. There were two large stable buildings with rear doors leading to their grazing pasture. As the wide gravel and dirt path continued north past the stables, there were separate blacksmith and brick-making buildings. Most plantations created a community of self-sufficiency. Next was a storage building where all the workmen would store supplies. The carpenter worked in the next building, and the carriage house was north of that. The Johnsons had three carriages of various sizes stored in the carriage house. Which one they used depended on the number of people who were traveling. The whole family could fit in the largest carriage, but it was a cozy fit.

One of the most important buildings was the cotton gin building in which the picked cotton was run through the mills to separate the seeds from the cotton fiber. This greatly quickened the speed in which cotton could be processed, fifty bales per day versus one bale by hand. Then the cotton was pressed down into bales. These bales were moved into the next building until it was full. Then they were stored in one of the warehouses near the river. When there was enough to ship, Father would contact a local shipper to transport. The Johnsons had a total of four cotton gins. Exporting had become more difficult due to the blockade in the Gulf of Mexico by the Union, but they still got it out. The last building was the smokehouse. It had become very important in lengthening how long they could keep meat before needing to eat it.

The next year, on March 4, 1862, a few slaves escaped, and their first stop was the house of Edwin and Marie. Marie was alone at the time as Edwin had gone to the primary house for the morning. The four escaped slaves were very angry and very strong. They were trying to find some money or valuables to help them along their travels north. They also wanted extra food for their trip. When they found Marie, she screamed. They went crazy since she wouldn't stop screaming. Their wonderful and sensitive Marie was found beaten and choked to death. Everyone was devastated. She was buried two days later in the family cemetery. Then Edwin took his anger out on the plantation slaves. There were unwarranted beatings and the withholding of food. This only led to more unrest and more slaves either escaping or attempting to escape.

Uncle Edwin grew ill again under the pressure of all the events of the last several months. He realized he would not get better and made the decision to teach Bella the workings of the plantation. As more slaves ran away, Uncle Edwin continued to fail. Finally, he died on October 29, 1862. So…there was Bella, totally unprepared for the situation she was now in but forced to do her best to help her family.

Part 2

The Union

Chapter 15

Prior to the Mexican War, the Army had fifty-six military posts in the United States of which only twelve were west of the Mississippi river. Treaties with Britain gained the California and Oregon territories, and the 1853 agreement with Mexico gained the southern Arizona and New Mexico territories. The Army had to move west.

By 1859, the US Army had seventy-six forts west of the Mississippi river. The Army divided the nation into seven military departments:

1. East—everything east of the Mississippi river. Headquartered in Washington, DC.
2. West—from Mississippi river to Rocky Mountains and Canada to Rio Grande. Headquartered in St. Louis, Missouri.
3. Oregon—Oregon and Washington territories. Headquartered in Fort Vancouver, Vancouver, Washington.
4. California—State of California and parts of Utah and New Mexico territories. Headquartered in San Francisco, California.
5. Utah—the parts of Utah not part of the California area. Headquartered in Camp Floyd, Utah.
6. New Mexico—New Mexico not part of the Calif area. Headquartered in Sante Fe, New Mexico.
7. Texas—whole state headquartered in San Antonio, Texas.

Each department was commanded by a brigadier general or colonel. The Army was reduced to fifteen regiments to man all seven departments. Western forts were primarily designed as shelter for small communities of officers, enlisted men, family members, and civilian followers and not defensive structures. They were built by the soldiers on site, so the quality would depend on the skills of those soldiers and materials available. All forts preferred lumber, but brick, stone, or adobe were used if lumber was unavailable.

The American West was so huge the Army was hard-pressed to maintain a presence everywhere they were needed. Most of the forts were only maintained by one to two companies meaning under two hundred men. Their primary purpose in the West was to protect civilians. A number of Army officers had little regard for the civilians on the frontier. They were struck by the low regard frontiersmen had for human life. Army officers wanted to resolve issues with the Indians with nonviolence, but civilians wanted more. The Army also broke up fights among the civilians themselves. Kansas and Missouri both had several conflicts needing Army intervention due to issues about permitting slavery or not in the five years prior to the Civil War.

Many officers lived comfortably in the east while the frontier men not so much. Most of the latter included young boys and men seeking adventure, escaping problems at home, and European immigrants. After the Mexican War, in 1848, the Army went to peacetime levels, which were below a total of ten thousand men. Due to the West expansion, the Army then grew to thirteen thousand by adding privates. Then in 1855, Congress added four additional regiments to the Army, which included three different mounted troops. The Dragons wore orange hats to distinguish them from the Mounted Riflemen, who wore green, and the Cavalry in yellow. Each also had different weapons.

Major Michael O'Malley was in command of a Cavalry unit after the Mexican War at Fort Riley in north central Kansas on the Kansas river. He helped fight the skirmishes with Native Indians. O'Malley was a tall man at 6'2" and a sturdy 200 pounds. He had light ash-brown hair and sea-blue eyes—some called them hazel—

and an easygoing manner. However, he could be very stern and had been in the US Army since the age of seventeen. He was born on May 25, 1829, in Cincinnati, Ohio.

By 1860, the Army had increased to sixteen thousand men, and it upgraded the standard infantry weapons from muskets to rifles. Although muzzle-loading rifled muskets remained the standard infantry weapon, the cavalry used breechloaders and repeating rifles. All US Army units started daily weapons practice to develop accuracy. This practice was tracked, and then the men were classified according to their ability. O'Malley's men were already good shots, but this target practice made them even better. He was delighted when Captain George McClellan went to Europe and developed a new saddle. This saddle was used by the Cavalry until after WWII.

Chapter 16

After leaving the Virginia Military Academy, Jonathan Johnson did not want to attend West Point like many of his classmates. Instead, he joined the US Army and moved quickly up the ranks due to his military training. He was stationed in the West Department at the headquarters in St. Louis, Missouri. He traveled to several forts, inspecting their situations and determining any needs. Then he would return to report his findings and arrange for those supplies to be shipped out. During some of his trips, he was able to get involved in the skirmishes that particular fort had to deal with. He didn't want to admit that he looked forward to these skirmishes because that is what he trained for. This was his assignment for two years.

Jonathan was able to go home to the plantation for one month before joining the Army and a year and a half later for another month. That was the year Bella turned sixteen years old. He greatly enjoyed his time at home. He was able to relax, enjoy Emma's cooking, tumble around with Marcus, and ride horseback in the fields. He continued to work with Bella on trapping and shooting, but they no longer hunted for deer. Several evenings his father, brother, and himself would sit in a parlor and discuss military strategies, events that happened while the boys had been at the Virginia Military Academy, and how the plantation was doing. On his trip for Bella's birthday, the three talked about the succession of all southern states and the creation of the Confederate States of America. Jonathan had different views than his father and brother, which eventually led to a loud discussion.

ANNABELLA'S STORY

Andrew started raising his voice, "The people up north have no right to tell us how to manage our plantations."

Then Jonathan responded in the same tone, "The people up north just don't want the slavery system to expand. Most of them do not own slaves and don't understand why it is needed. They hire and pay all of their workers."

Andrew's voice got louder as he stood, putting his hands on his hips. "So what are all the plantation owners supposed to do with all their slaves and the money they have spent on those slaves?"

Then Jonathan stood and took a step toward Andrew. As he was much taller but Andrew was broader, their father was very concerned about what could happen next.

Father said, "Boys. That is enough. Let's agree to disagree."

Father had ended it and they all agreed to not discuss this topic anymore.

Jonathan had come home in his Army uniform for Bella's birthday and was somewhat surprised at all the looks and comments he received while traveling. He soon realized that it may be better not to wear it the deeper South he went. His uniform was blue clothing made of high quality wool and silver buttons down the front. The jacket was a darker shade of blue, somewhere between navy and royal blue, while the pants were a lighter shade, usually close to sky blue. Wool was warm but itchy and hot in the South. Johnathan, like most soldiers, wore cotton shirts and undergarments usually brought or shipped from home. He wore one but many wore two black straps across his chest for equipment. He kept his black belt with its silver buckle and boots shiny and clean. When he was at formal affairs, he wore a red sash around his waist. Jonathan was happy he was not in the sharpshooter corps as they wore forest-green uniforms during battle for camouflage. He did not like those uniforms, but he was a good shot. Anyway, like most soldiers, Jonathan carried his gun, a Model 1861 North Springfield rifle.

Their weapons included a scabbard, a long sword, and this model 1861 with a bayonet made in Springfield, Massachusetts. It was favored for its range, accuracy, and reliability. It had a weight of nine pounds and a range of two hundred to four hundred yards. However, a marksman could hit a man up to five hundred yards away. A good rifleman, which Jonathan was, could fire two to three shots per minute. A Cavalry soldier usually carried a single-shot breech loading rifle. They could fire four to six shots per minute. One negative was this model was scarce early in the war, and most soldiers used smoothbore Model 1862 muskets. Eventually, over one million Model 1861 rifles were produced by contracting out production to other firms in the Union.

Upon his return to St. Louis, he was immediately assigned to Major Michael O'Malley. Companies were pulled together, and they headed east. O'Malley was in command of the Ohio First, Fifth, and Ninth Infantry companies under Colonel Alexander M. McCook. Jonathan had been promoted from first lieutenant to captain and was assigned to the Ninth Infantry company as this unit had just lost their captain to retirement.

Some of the other officers in his troop had gone to West Point. By 1861, 750 of the 1063 West Point graduates still living were on active service in the Army and 75 percent of the Army's 1,098 officers were West Point grads. Union generals Sherman, Bragg, and Grant were West Point graduates. They had left the Army but returned for the Civil War as they were not successful in civilian life.

Most of the regular Army were loyal to the Union. Officers, however, were split; of the West Point graduates, 168 were confederates, 556 union, and 26 took no active part in the war as they had mixed feelings about who to support. Of the officers in the Army, 20 percent of them resigned in 1861 to join the Confederacy. This kind of split was affecting not only the West Point grads and the US

ANNABELLA'S STORY

Army but every aspect of everyday life. People in the states through the middle of the country from east to west were the hardest hit with tension on what was right. But in every state, regardless of where, families argued.

Chapter 17

Major Michael O'Malley's State of Ohio played a key role in providing troops, military officers, and supplies to the Union Army. Due to its central location in the Northern United States and burgeoning population, Ohio was both politically and logistically important to the war effort. The third most populous state in the Union at the time, Ohio raised nearly 320,000 soldiers for the Union Army. The state was spared many of the horrors of war as only two minor battles were fought within its borders. Morgan's Raid in the summer of 1863 spread fear but little damage. Otherwise, Ohio troops fought in nearly every major campaign during the war.

As battles continued, Captain Jonathan Johnson saw more action than he would have wanted with these Ohio regiments. Officers could rank up by brevet during the war. A brevet was awarded for gallantry in battle. Entitled officers wore the insignia of increased rank, but there was no increase in pay. For Example, Robert E. Lee, a captain, received three brevets in Mexico allowing him to wear the rank of colonel for many years prior to official promotion. Later, he resigned from the US Army to take command of the state military forces of Virginia. Due to these field brevets, Major O'Malley became a colonel commanding the Fifth Ohio Regiment, which had a total of eight companies. Captain Johnson became a Major, commanding two companies. His four fellow officers, all captains, commanded another six among them. Jonathan also had a first lieutenant and two master sergeants for his two companies totaling two-hundred-five men. The other captains had at least one to two sergeants and up to ninety to one hundred men per company. New recruits were added periodically, which helped replenish those no longer able to fight. The Cavalry units, commanded by two of the other captains, would "negotiate" with people near their encampments to release quality horses when one of theirs died. They were also good at getting a local blacksmith to fix or make new rigging for their horses. When they found both a good carpenter and blacksmith in the same place, work would be done to fix artillery equipment and repair rifles if possible. The deeper south they moved, the more "unwilling" the locals were to assist. Having lived in the South, Jonathan usually took the lead in talking to the southerners. He spoke their "language."

In early 1863, Colonel O'Malley and his regiment, between eight to nine-hundred men, were to head to Mississippi. They were part of the Union Army that took Baton Rouge, Louisiana. As in most battles, there were many wounded and a lot of blood. Jonathan would lie awake many nights still hearing the sounds of anguish from the wounded on both sides. Their cries, moans, and the whimpering were never ending. Several soldiers lost hands, feet, or their entire limb. Some would have chunks of flesh removed from cannon fire or grenades, and the doctors would sew up what was left. Others lost eyes, ears, a few fingers and toes. Johnathan now understood why Michael talked of ways to deal with the sights and sounds no one should have to see or hear. Many soldiers with less serious wounds would continue to fight, and those that recovered from more serious ones wanted to return to their units. Jonathan was a strong believer in saying a prayer before each fight and going to see the wounded, giving them encouraging words at the end of each day. Michael liked this practice and encouraged his other officers to do the same. The men really appreciated this practice, knowing that it was done sincerely and not a required task. This inspired all the soldiers, and they were very loyal to their commander.

One night, when Colonel Michael O'Malley had a few homemade brews, he talked of his time in the Mexican War. The horrors he described even made seasoned soldiers cringe. The Mexicans were savage fighters, and unfortunately, some of the US soldiers became ones as well. The only positive result was learning a few new military maneuvers, but they never wanted to behave like the ones they fought.

They were then directed to head to Vicksburg, Mississippi. This would be the second battle at Vicksburg. As Colonel O'Malley and the troop approached Vicksburg in May 1863, they needed a place to camp. With hesitation, Major Johnson informed the colonel, his family's plantation was very close to their destination. He agreed to head there for their encampment. Jonathan did not know the state of affairs on the plantation at that time, but he was looking forward to seeing some family members.

Part 3

The Confederacy

Chapter 18

Soon after the Johnson sons were back at their military posts, John knew the very serious events of the last few months were coming to a head. States had started to succeed from the United State of America. Between December 20, 1860, and February 1, 1861, South Carolina, Mississippi, Florida, Alabama, Georgia, Louisiana, and Texas had all left the Union. The Southern states were anticipating that Abraham Lincoln would become the next president of the United States. His views on slavery were not in line with the ways of the South. The country was moving west, and Lincoln did not want slavery to move west with it.

They were structured with a plantation system to grow crops, lots of crops, and especially cotton. And this system needed more labor than could be hired, so it relied on enslaved Americans of African descent for labor. Most Southern leaders and plantation owners believed in white supremacy and that Negroes were not equal to Whites. The thought was that the Negroes' natural and normal condition were to be slaves. John Johnson did not necessarily agree with these strong views of his fellow southerners, but what choice did he have but to fight? He needed those slaves to work the fields. If only the other owners were more humane, maybe things wouldn't have gotten to this point.

The Confederate States of America were officially formed on February 8, 1861. They had a House of Representatives and a Senate and elected Jefferson Davis as their president. Ten years prior, in 1851, Davis had resigned from the US Senate to run unsuccessfully for governor of Mississippi. Two years later, President Franklin Pierce appointed Davis as secretary of war. During his tenure, Davis focused on increasing the Army's size and improving national defenses and weapons technology as well as providing protection for settlers in the Western territories. Jefferson's efforts were well advised for his then country as secretary of war but were a detriment for the Southern states during the Civil War.

United States of America President Abraham Lincoln

Confederate States of America President Jefferson Davis

ANNABELLA'S STORY

Abraham Lincoln was elected president and inaugurated on March 4, 1861. Then on April 12, 1861, a Confederate attack took place on Fort Sumter, a Union fort in Charleston, South Carolina. As the other states had succeeded, the Confederate soldiers seized control of all federal arsenals and forts but did allow those officers and men that wanted to travel north. When Fort Sumter wouldn't surrender, it was attacked. In response, President Lincoln called up the troops on April 15, 1861, and the war had begun.

More states succeeded. Between April 17, 1861, and May 20, 1861, Virginia, Arkansas, Tennessee, and North Carolina all joined the cause. Kentucky and Missouri were part of the Confederacy though their territories were largely controlled by the North after 1862. Arizona and New Mexico territories supported the South as they wanted slavery to move west. Lastly, there were two of the five civilized Indian tribes who fought with the South, the Choctaw and Chickasaw.

Although the South produced most of the cotton in the Americas, most of the mills that made the cloth were in the North. This made getting material for uniforms and other clothing more difficult in the beginning for both sides and as the war progressed even more so. In general, Confederate uniforms were gray, but the majority wore mixed shades of brown and khaki. The officer uniforms, like Colonel Johnson's, were gray and double-breasted with gold buttons. The jackets were short-waisted and the pants were heavy cotton denim. Most of the soldiers wore cotton shirts and undergarments from home. They, like the North, had black belts and a black strap over their chests to carry equipment. The black belts had gold buckles, and there were gold decals on their sleeves. During special events, John and other officers wore yellow scarves around their waists. Most wore black boots, and all carried Enfield 1853 rifles with bayonets. The Enfields were British rifles made and assembled at the Tower of London, England. The British sold to both sides with 900,000 P53 rifles imported by the Americas; the Union received 505,000 and the Confederates 300,000.

Soldiers on both sides carried a total of thirty to forty pounds of gear. The left shoulder usually carried the gun, bayonet, and scabbard. The bayonet was carried separately from the rifle to reduce the chance of someone accidentally getting stabbed. The belt held a leather cartridge box with the ammunition. The right shoulder usually carried a pouch of food and a canteen of water or coffee. Left-handed soldiers switched shoulders. Unlike the North, who carried knapsacks, Confederate soldiers rolled extra clothing, shaving items, and possibly a shelter half in their blanket. As the war progressed, Confederates were known to take equipment, shoes, and clothing from dead Union soldiers. Taking clothing had mixed results; it could get you shot by a fellow soldier, or you could sneak up on the enemy in disguise. Both John and Andrew would only allow their men to take equipment and other supplies they needed. They reprimanded those that took valuables and would even whip those that tortured severely wounded Northern soldiers. They needed to maintain their humanity.

The first battle of the war, First Battle of Bull Run, was in Virginia in July, 1861. The Union had marched on Richmond, Virginia, the new Confederate capital, but were defeated. The South, however, were exhausted and both sides suffered losses as they were ill-trained this early in the war. Instead of pressing on and pushing the North further back, they stayed, giving the North time to regroup. Soon after, the Union blockaded the eastern coast and the Gulf of Mexico. In response, the South built smaller vessels that could outmaneuver the enemy. But being outnumbered, the Union was in New Orleans, Louisiana, by early May 1862. Taking this city is how General Grant and other Union soldiers could move north along the Mississippi river.

The railroads were important to both sides for troop and supply movement. The South's most important lines were the Richmond, Fredericksburg, and Potomac railroads. The Baltimore and Ohio railroads suffered great damage as they were taken, retaken, destroyed, and rebuilt several times during advances and retreats. Both sides also used telegraph lines to communicate, first the South and later the North. The Confederates used signal flags on the battlefield, and the Union used hot-air balloons to observe troop movement.

Chapter 19

Major John Johnson, Bella's father, soon became Colonel Johnson and was part of the Mississippi regiments that reported to Lieutenant General John C. Pemberton. When volunteers were called for, over eighty thousand white men volunteered to join from Mississippi. His regiment, the Fifth Mississippi Infantry Regiment, usually fought with the First Battalion Sharpshooters and Third Mississippi Cavalry Regiment. The commanders did not know each other prior to the war but became close friends and confidants during it. First Lieutenant Andrew Johnson moved up to Captain Johnson and commanded one of the ten companies under his Father. Each company consisted of eighty to one hundred men. That number changed up and down during battles and as new recruiters were brought in.

John's unit fought several skirmishes, but in late 1862, Union's General Grant wanted to take the city of Vicksburg. General Pemberton was tasked to defend the city. Vicksburg was on a high hill and had been fortified. It was important to the South that Vicksburg be held; it blocked the Union from traveling down the Mississippi river and had become a hub for the movement of supplies to the South. Grant led his troops from the South, New Orleans, Louisiana, and General Sherman led his troops from the North. General Hovey also led a group east from Arkansas. On August 5, 1862, General Grant had taken Baton Rouge. When the Confederates couldn't retake it, they retreated to Vicksburg. This included Colonel Johnson's unit. When the Confederates were able to cut off General Grant's supply lines, he had to retreat. Meanwhile, General Sherman had a difficult time maneuvering through the swampy land and, when he finally was close to the city, took heavy losses trying to climb the hill. Sherman incurred 1,700 casualties, while the Confederates only had 76. General Hovey never made it there at all.

Unfortunately, Andrew was one of the seventy-six injured during the battle. His left hand was badly damaged, and the surgeon removed it just above the wrist. It took six weeks for it to heal enough for Andrew to return to combat. At the time his hand was injured, he continued to command his men until it was clear the Union forces were in retreat. While he was in recovery, he continued to work with his unit on maneuvers and sending out scouting parties. After his remaining skin was healed, one of his men helped him affix a kind of hook so he could still hold a gun for shooting. With some practice, he could at least hit what he aimed at and reload, but the second action took more time than most men.

Andrew missed the rest of his family, his sweet but irritating sisters, and his little cute, rowdy baby brother. Most of all he longed to see his loving mother—her sunshiny hair, very sky-blue eyes, and especially her smile. He wrote home every other week until recently. He would write about where they were and things he saw and comment on what he thought they were doing at home. Andrew received a few letters from home, but it was difficult to get letters through. On the other hand, his men loved him, and they would follow him wherever he led them. He was masterful with military strategy, which kept his men safe, and they could cause more casualties to the enemy. Andrew focused on these two functions, wanting his men to go home to their families.

Colonel John felt more pressure than his son. He was responsible for a lot of men, and to be a good commander, he along with his fellow senior officers had to think of the men as pieces on a chessboard. Decisions were harder, but they were necessary to win this war. He also worried about his family back on the plantation. Were they doing well? Was Edwin keeping all the slaves in line? John wrote home and sent his letters along with Andrew's. Although they were in the general area of Vicksburg, the Plantation was often eighty to one hundred miles from where he was fighting, and when they were

ANNABELLA'S STORY

closer, he could not just leave his post. Mary, his loving wife, did not do well when things were not going well. He protected her, like most men, from all the duties of the plantation and any financial issues. She was just a beautiful petite woman and his joy for living. John longed to hold her again.

John worried about his oldest son, how he could have stayed with the US Army. John knew there were many families that had split alliances and were torn apart just like the United States was. He did not approve of how some plantation owners treated their slaves, but without the slaves, how would any of them run their fields? The northern states had no right to dictate how the southern states should operate. The South didn't tell the North how to run their factories or build their houses, towns, and railroads. It was unfair, so he had little option but to fight with others from his state of Mississippi and the surrounding states. John also knew that if they did not have a quick end to the fighting, the North definitely had an advantage. They outnumbered the South four to one in military forces, and the North also had superior military equipment, industrial facilities, and railroads.

As the North finally got their footing and moved through the South, they freed the slaves at each plantation. Some of the slaves would stay and fight; others moved North, while a few stayed with their previous owners due to loyalty. The loyal group was the smallest and usually consisted of the domestic slaves as they felt closer to the families. The North were also able to get stored cotton in Southern warehouses back up North as some of the factories were shut down due to the lack of material. When the war started, the Confederate states, excluding Missouri, Kentucky, and Arizona, totaled just over nine million residents. However, over 3.5 million of those were slaves.

General Pemberton and his men fought in the surrounding area of Vicksburg, always leaving enough men to defend the city and fight off any Northerners in the area. Their next big battle started in early 1863. Union soldiers fought the Confederates in the Battle of Jackson, Mississippi. Although Jackson was small, it was a strategic center for manufacturing and moving supplies to the troops. General Sherman took the town of Jackson after a couple of days of fighting.

When the South tried to take it back, they failed and again were forced to retreat to Vicksburg. Soon would come the Second Battle of Vicksburg.

Chapter 20

It was early morning when Union Officer Colonel O'Malley and troops approached the Johnson Plantation. Raymond was the first to see them and was very concerned about what having Union soldiers on the property would mean. He immediately sought out Bella, who stood for several seconds, dumbstruck. She asked Raymond to get Big George, and together they walked out to meet the oncoming group. Bella was approached by several men on horseback. Behind them were many, many men. She stood in the middle of the drive and made fists to help control her shakiness. What would the soldiers do to the family, the house, the livestock? Everything could be at risk. One of the men started to speak.

"Miss, my name is Colonel Michael O'Malley, and we request access to the property for our troops," he said in a firm and confident voice.

Bella replied, "A proper gentleman would never talk to the owner of a property from upon a horse. Do they not have gentlemen in the North?"

A few seconds later, O'Malley dismounted, removed his hat, and slowly strode forward to greet Bella properly. Two other men also dismounted but did not approach. Bella thought about how tall O'Malley was and, for just a few seconds, how handsome he was.

O'Malley said, "My apologies, I am requesting that we have access to your property."

He then waited for Bella to respond.

Bella said, "Do I really have a choice in this matter, or will you do it anyway?"

Both of them stood quietly for a few seconds just looking at each other. Both of them felt a strange attraction. They both thought, *This can't be happening.*

Bella said, "There are plenty of empty fields you can camp in as there are no more slaves to work them. But I have some conditions."

At that moment, a man approached and took off his hat. Bella wasn't sure which emotion to feel first, joy, anger, happiness, or sadness. There before her eyes was her big brother Jonathan. She stood there not sure what she should do, but within ten seconds, she gave in to the happiness and leaped into his arms crying. Jonathan hugged her tight and whispered that everything would be all right. Bella released him and turned to address O'Malley again, tears running down her face but joy in her eyes.

Bella said, "This is my list of requests."

1. There is to be no taking of livestock or food stuff without consent. The plantation will provide food provisions but at a rationed rate.
2. There is to be no wandering of soldiers unless specifically on patrol.
3. There is to be no interference with the work around the plantation.
4. Only officers are allowed in the main house unless messages were being sent.
5. All workers on the plantation will be treated with respect.

She did not think the last request would be a problem. Weren't the northerners supposed to like slaves and want them free?

O'Malley nodded as she made each request.

O'Malley asked, "Is there anything else, Miss Johnson?"

Bella said, "Yes. Could my brother be the one responsible for ensuring the requests were followed?" O'Malley and Jonathan glanced at each other, and both nodded.

ANNABELLA'S STORY

Bella indicated that Big George would direct them to fields that would be suitable for their needs and where fresh water could be found. She also told him that someone should come and tell Raymond what foodstuff was needed. Her last statement was to ask how many officers would need beds in the main house. O'Malley said he would let her know soon. Unbeknownst to Bella, Colonel Michael O'Malley continued to be surprised at how taken he was with Bella. What an attractive and brave young woman. Did she have the same colored eyes as he did? Both men returned to their horses, and all three men on the ground started to follow Big George on foot. The rest of the soldiers on horseback also dismounted and walked on. As Bella turned to go back into the house, Jonathan called after her to not tell anyone he was here until it could come up to the house himself. She winked at him and went on her way.

Upon returning to the house, Mother, the other children, Emma, Ellie, and Mimi were all standing there in great anticipation. When she told them that a large group of Union soldiers would be staying with them for a few days, no one spoke. She told them not to worry; everything would be all right, and she smiled as those were the words Jonathan had said. Big George and Bella had already completed their morning inspection, and now it was time for late breakfast. Everyone was chatting excitedly at the table, and little eating was actually taking place. Mother tried to start the children's lesson, but it was a no go. Soon, she gave up, and they all walked outside to watch the activity.

In about an hour, five men walked at a steady pace toward the house. As they came closer into sight, Mother stood and put her hand up to shield the sunlight. A few minutes later, she gasped and put her hands to her mouth. Then Mother screamed with joy and started running toward the men. It wasn't long before the two younger girls also started running. Marcus was confused; he did not understand what everyone was so excited about. Bella came up beside Marcus and leaned down to whisper in his ear that it was his brother Jonathan. Marcus looked up at her, paused, and he too started running and screaming. Jonathan walked a little faster, and within a minute or two, the entire group was hugging, laughing, and jumping around. The scene brought tears to Bella's eyes as well as the three slave women. The other soldiers stopped where they were to give the family reunion some time alone.

With a little difficulty, Jonathan got the family to calm down, and together they walked toward the house. Raymond had come around the corner of the house, hearing all the commotion. He too smiled with his missing teeth, crossed his arms, and gave a little chuckle. There were few happy moments anymore, and everyone needed to enjoy them when they occurred. Jonathan followed the family into the house, while Raymond walked to the other four men. Raymond's group had a list of supplies they needed and asked if he could help. The men were very polite, which was not something Raymond was used to from white men, but he did need to know how many days they would be staying and how many men were on site. It was going to be at least a week, and there were about 850 men. The soldiers told him what they had on hand, and they agreed on food for the day. Raymond called the other slave men over to lead the various soldiers to the locations needed. He knew he would need to discuss this with Bella as they would be using up a lot of food very quickly. Although Raymond could not read well, he could read numbers, and he saw big ones on the paper. One of the soldiers did say that they would go hunting each morning they were in the camp. Raymond told him that he would indicate the best places to hunt.

Chapter 21

Raymond found Bella in one of the parlors with the rest of the family. He motioned that he needed her, and she politely left the room. They walked to the library, which was where Bella kept all the ledgers. Raymond gave Bella the list of all the food supplies the soldiers had requested and that they would go hunting every day they were in camp. The quantity was too much, and it would wipe them out, leaving little while they waited for new crops to mature. Next, they agreed on what they could give up, and Bella wrote it all down. Then she asked Raymond to give a message to Colonel O'Malley that she would like to meet with him this evening or tomorrow to discuss the food situation. She hoped he would be reasonable.

When Bella returned to the parlor, the situation was much calmer, and Jonathan moved toward Bella to talk to her. They also walked into the library for their discussion. Jonathan reviewed the room assignments. The first floor had eight rooms; the dining room, large foyer, and front parlor were across the front. The food prep room, music room, and ballroom were across the middle of the house. The ballroom extended to the back of the house and was the largest room in the house. The balance of the rear of the house was the library and rear parlor. The dining room, front parlor, back parlor, and ballroom all had French doors leading to the front and rear porches. There were Greek-style columns in the front and both front and rear balconies above the porches. The second floor had ten rooms with the area over the foyer open. As the staircase was wide and the railings were ornate in design, the foyer was magnificent in appearance. There were four bedrooms on the left side of the house of which both Jonathan and Andrew had rooms and the other two were left open for guests. Beyond the foyer, there was a room for storage and two smaller rooms side by side behind that one. There was a small bedroom Marcus was currently using and a sitting room to the left of it. Marcus liked to use it as his playroom. On the right side front to back were two more bedrooms, slightly larger than the ones on the left, in which Bella stayed in the front room and Margaret and Lizzie shared the next. A few years earlier, the shared room had been shared by all three girls, and the front bedroom was left open for guests. This had given them a total of three rooms for overnight guests. The last bedroom was the master bedroom and was the largest bedroom in the house. Mother continued to stay in this room awaiting her husband's return. The two front bedrooms and the outside back bedrooms also had French doors leading onto the balconies. There was a third set of doors behind the little sitting room, so anyone on the second floor could access the rear balcony.

Jonathan let Bella know that there would be ten officers needing a place to sleep, if possible, including himself. Bella suggested

ANNABELLA'S STORY

that Marcus could move into Mother's room, and she and her sisters could share hers. Depending how they wanted to sleep, one or three men could sleep in each of the first floor parlors. That would give six open bedrooms. Jonathan thought they should have all his sisters in the middle bedroom and he would take the one where Marcus slept so they could feel safe having him near. He wanted to put his colonel in the front bedroom Bella was currently in so he could go out on the balcony. Bella then asked Jonathan to attend the meeting she had asked for to discuss the food supplies and the issues to be resolved. They both stood, Jonathan saying he wanted to discuss what had happened over the past two years and that he needed to get back to his men. She said that she was so happy he was here and gave him another giant hug.

The next morning, Bella, Jonathan, and Michael all met in the dining room to talk.

"Ms. Johnson, I understand you wanted to talk to me about some details," Michael started.

Bella replied, "Yes, I would like to discuss your food requirements. Big George and I have reviewed your requests and the amount you requested is too much. It would deplete our supplies within two weeks and leave us with little to last until the next harvest. And by the way, you can call me Bella."

Michael said, "I understand. Do you have any suggestions?"

Bella nodded, saying, "Yes, here is a list of what we can give you as long as you do not stay here past four weeks, Colonel."

"You can call me Michael. May I see the list?" Michael said as he reached for the paper.

Michael scanned the list, saying, "Let me review this with one of my lieutenants. I am sure we can make this work. Is there anything else?"

Bella finished with "No, not at this time. Thank you, Colonel… Michael."

They smiled at each other, and Jonathan came over to pat her on the back and whisper that she was handling this very well.

As Michael left, Jonathan stayed to talk to Bella, and he quizzed, "Where is Uncle Edwin?"

Bella answered, "He and Marie have died. Uncle Edwin died almost a year ago, he was very sick and Marie…" Bella lowered her head then continued, "She was killed by some runaway slaves. After that is when Uncle Edwin got sick and most of the slaves left."

Jonathan spoke softly, "So YOU are running the plantation?"

Bella nodded as she said, "Uncle Edwin showed me things during his last six months. Then Raymond and Big George had to teach me other things I needed to know."

"That is amazing but must be stressful," Jonathan replied.

Bella continued by saying, "Yes, but now we have a routine. I suppose that will change with all of you here."

Jonathan finished with "I suppose it will. I will make sure things don't get too crazy."

The pair chatted for a few more minutes. Bella gave a box to Jonathan with all the letters she had written and not sent, then they each went on to do their respective tasks. Jonathan turned and then talked about Bandit, the mastiff. He had worked with him during his times at home. They got along well; Jonathan wanted to take Bandit to where the troops were to guard the horses. There were too many horses to all fit in the stables, so most were tied up along a tree line. Bella did remind him that Bandit did not like many people, especially men, so he better warn his men. Bella also decided to let Raymond know the other two dogs were not to be unleashed.

The next two days were spent with the soldiers hunting and butchering their allotted amount of livestock. The men were very polite as of now, and Bella hoped this behavior would continue, but she was unfamiliar with how people reacted under pressure. The rest of the residents on the plantation continued to work as always, and the Union officers met two to three times each day for discussions. During those days, everyone started realizing how Colonel Michael and Bella were often seen chatting and giving each other passing glances. Was something happening here?

Michael smiled, saying, "Miss Bella, how are you doing today?"

Bella blushed slightly, replying, "Very well, thank you. Did you enjoy your breakfast?"

ANNABELLA'S STORY

"It was delicious. Please thank Emma for me—she is a wonderful cook," Michael said as he rubbed his stomach.

Bella responded, "I will. Maybe I will see you later?"

"I certainly hope so," Michael said with a wink.

They were both smiling that smile that those in love smile. Everyone in the household, or at least the adults, thought it was so precious. It was Bella's first love.

Chapter 22

O'Malley and his officers met with General Grant and the other officers in Grant's command about two days after their arrival to the plantation. The defensive line around Vicksburg ran for approximately six and a half miles based on terrain of varying elevations that included hills and knobs with steep slopes, which would require an attacker to ascend them under fire. The perimeter included many gun pits, forts, trenches, redoubts, and lunettes. A redoubt is a smaller fort consisting of an enclosed defensive emplacement outside the main fort. Some were made on earthworks, while others were constructed of stone and brick. It would protect soldiers outside the main defensive line. Earlier, the soldiers made permanent structures known as a lunette. It was an angularly built shape usually positioned at the corner of a fort. A lunette would then be developed into a redan. Redans were a feature of fortification in a V-shaped salient angle toward an expected attack. Like redoubts, some were made from earthworks and others of stone. All of these reinforcements had been built according to Captain Andrew Johnson's instructions. Again, his excellent military strategy was helping to keep them safe.

The major fortifications of the city included Fort Hill, on a high bluff north of the city; the Stockade Redan, dominating the approach to the city on Graveyard Road from the northeast; the Third Louisiana Redan; the Great Redoubt; the Railroad Redoubt, protecting the gap for the railroad line entering the city; the Square Fort (Fort Garrott); a salient along the Hall's Ferry Road; and the South Fort. Captain Johnson's unit would man the Stockade Redan.

There were over thirty thousand soldiers in the city, and each fortification was well manned.

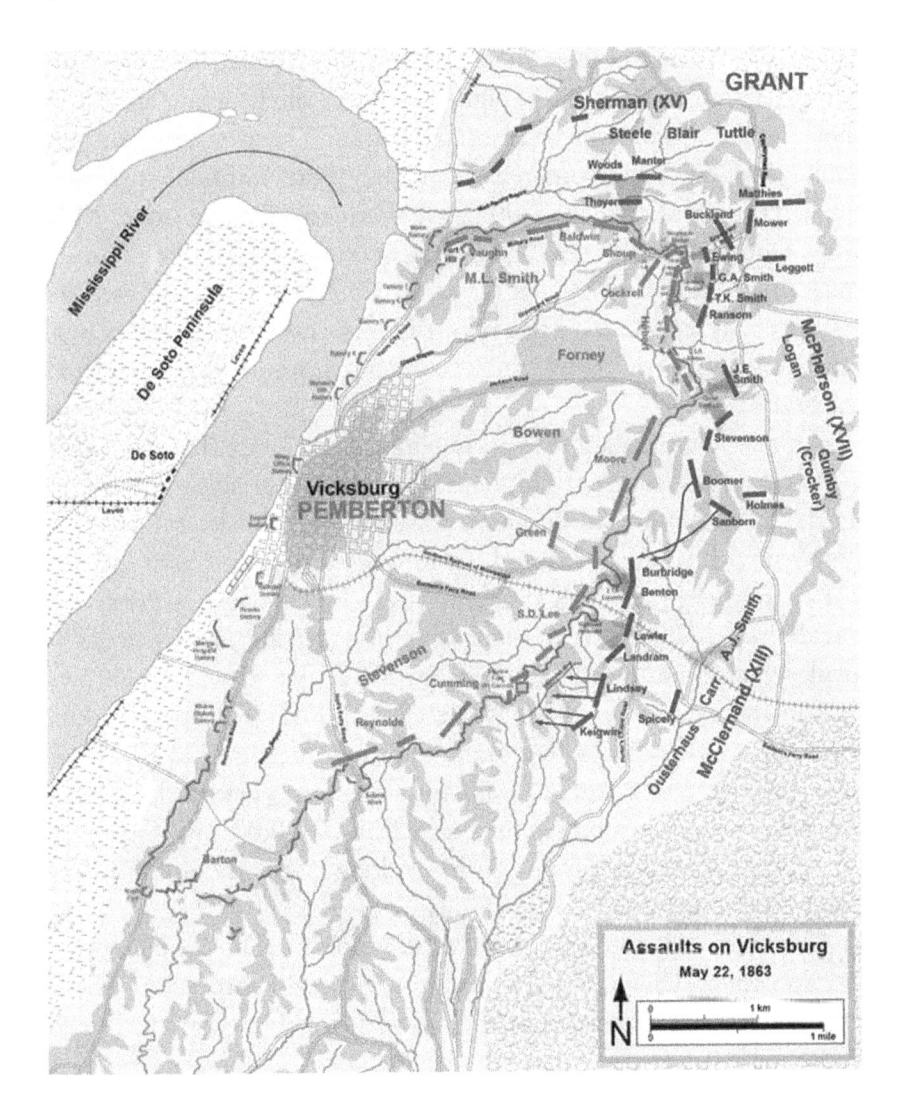

Grant wanted to overwhelm the Confederates before they could fully organize their defenses and ordered an assault against the Stockade Redan in Vicksburg for May 19, 1863. Troops from Sherman's corps had a difficult time approaching the position under rifle and artillery fire from the Thirty-Sixth Mississippi Infantry as they had in the first battle. They had to negotiate a steep ravine protected by abatis, a field fortification consisting of the branches of trees laid in a row with the sharpened tops directed outward, toward the enemy. The trees were then interlaced with wire. Sherman also had to cross a six-foot-deep, eight-foot-wide ditch before attacking the seventeen-foot-high walls of the redan. The first attempt was easily repulsed. Grant ordered an artillery bombardment to soften the defenses, and at about 2:00 p.m., Sherman's division under Maj. Gen. Francis P. Blair tried again, but only a small number of men were able to advance even as far as the ditch below the redan. The assault collapsed in an exchange of rifle fire and hand grenades lobbing back and forth. Again, the Union had far greater casualties than the South.

Grant planned another assault for May 22 but this time with greater care; his troops would first reconnoiter thoroughly and soften up the defenses with artillery and naval gunfire. The lead units were supplied with ladders to ascend the fortification walls. Grant did not want a long siege, and this attack was to be by the entire Army across a wide front. Union forces bombarded the city all night, from 220 artillery pieces and naval gunfire from Rear Adm. David D. Porter's fleet in the Mississippi river. While causing little property damage, they damaged Confederate morale. On the morning of May 22, the defenders were bombarded again for four hours before the Union attacked once more along a three-mile front at 10:00 am.

Colonel John Johnson said to Andrew, "Son, the union is not going to stop until they take this city."

Andrew replied, "Father, we must hold out. The people of this city are afraid. They are talking of hiding in caves with all this shelling. But we keep repelling them. Do you still think they will keep attacking?"

John continued, "There can be no doubt. Those blue bellies want control of the Mississippi. They will never stop until they either kill us all or we surrender."

Sherman attacked once again down the Graveyard Road, with 150 volunteers leading the way with ladders and planks, followed by the other divisions arranged in a long column of regiments. They hoped to achieve a breakthrough by concentrating their mass on a narrow front. They were driven back in the face of heavy rifle fire. A few brigades made it as far as a ridge one hundred yards from Green's Redan, the southern edge of the Stockade Redan, from where they poured heavy fire into the Confederate position but to no avail. But the division behind them, waiting its turn to advance, did not have an opportunity to move forward.

O'Malley's corps were assigned to attack the center along the Jackson Road. They advanced to within one hundred yards of the Confederate line but halted to avoid dangerous flanking fire from Green's Redan. They took several casualties but only three deaths. Another brigade made it as far as the slope of the redan but huddled there, dodging grenades until dark, when they were recalled. When one of the brigades advanced in two columns against the redoubt, their attack also failed when they found their ladders were too short to scale the fortification walls. Andrew and his men had a little chuckle at short ladders. Stupid blue bellies.

On the Union left, corps moved along the Baldwin Ferry Road and astride the Southern Railroad of Mississippi. One division was assigned to capture the Railroad Redoubt and the Second Texas Lunette, while another division was assigned the Square Fort. The railroad division achieved a small breakthrough at the Second Texas Lunette and requested reinforcements. By 11:00 a.m., it was clear that a breakthrough was not forthcoming and that the advances by Sherman and McPherson were failures.

Sherman ordered two more assaults. At 2:15 p.m., troops moved out and were repulsed immediately. At 3:00 p.m., one of the divisions suffered so many casualties in their aborted advance that Sherman told them, "This is murder—order those troops back." More attempts were tried, but everything failed. All the divisions took great losses. Union casualties for the day totaled 502 killed, 2,550 wounded, and 147 missing, about evenly divided across the three corps fighting. Confederate casualties were estimated to have been under 500. Andrew still found it hard to believe the North would continue this slaughter of their own forces.

Grant reluctantly settled into a siege. Federal troops began to dig in, constructing elaborate entrenchments, which the soldiers of the time referred to as *ditches*. These surrounded the city and moved steadily closer to the Confederate fortifications with their backs against the Mississippi River and Union gunboats firing from the river.

Chapter 23

Confederate soldiers and citizens alike were trapped. General Pemberton was directed to surrender to save his men but he refused. President Davis had once told him the Confederacy must hold Vicksburg. General Pemberton was determined to hold his few miles of the Mississippi as long as possible, hoping for relief. Colonel Johnson advised him that this was not going to end well if it lasted very long.

A new problem confronted the Confederates. The dead and wounded of Grant's army lay in the heat of Mississippi summer, the odor of the deceased men and horses fouling the air, the wounded crying for medical help and water. These sounds brought back horrid memories for John Johnson as he had witnessed these events before. Grant first refused a request of truce, thinking it a show of weakness. Finally he relented, and the Confederates held their fire, while the Union recovered the wounded and dead on May 25, 1863. Soldiers from both sides mingled and traded as if no hostilities existed for the moment.

General Pemberton's outlook on escape was pessimistic, but there were still roads leading south out of Vicksburg unguarded by Union troops. Grant sought help from the Union general-in-chief. And they quickly began to shift Union troops in the West to meet Grant's needs. The first of these reinforcements was a five-thousand-man division from the Department of the Missouri on June 11. Next came a three-division detachment from XVI Corps on June 12, assembled from troops at the nearby posts of Corinth, Memphis, and LaGrange. The final significant group of reinforcements to join was the eight-thousand-strong IX Corps from the Department of the Ohio, arriving on June 14. With this last arrival, Grant had 77,000 men around Vicksburg. O'Malley's men intermixed with this last group, and as many knew each other, some came back to the plantation to share meals.

In an effort to cut Grant's supply line, Confederates in Louisiana attacked Milliken's Bend up the Mississippi on June 7. This was largely defended by recently enlisted United States colored troops. Despite having inferior weaponry, they fought bravely and repulsed the Confederates with help from gunboats, although at heavy cost; the defenders lost 652 to the Confederate 185. The loss at Milliken's Bend left the Confederates with little hope for relief.

Pemberton was boxed in with plentiful munitions but little food. The poor diet was telling on the Confederate soldiers. By the end of June, half were sick or hospitalized. Scurvy, malaria, dysentery, diarrhea, and other diseases cut their ranks. At least one city resident had to stay up at night to keep starving soldiers out of his vegetable garden. The constant shelling did not bother Pemberton as much as the loss of his food. As the siege wore on, fewer and fewer horses, mules, and dogs were seen wandering about Vicksburg. Shoe leather became a last resort of sustenance for many adults. Heavy artillery pieces were used by the Union in order to force the besieged city and its defenders into surrender.

John and Andrew spoke again with John, saying, "Andrew, the men are so hungry, and their sicknesses are causing great anguish. They will not last much longer. I fear what may happen next. Desperate men do desperate things."

Andrew replied, "Father, you and I are not doing well ourselves. Can you convince General Pemberton that it is time to surrender? They surely wouldn't send this many of us to prison camps. Wouldn't they just parole us? If so, the men could recover and return to fighting. We must do something."

As John nodded, he said, "Yes, we must do something."

During the siege, Union gunboats lobbed over 22,000 shells into the town, and Army artillery fire was even heavier. As the bar-

ANNABELLA'S STORY

rages continued, suitable housing in Vicksburg was reduced to a minimum. A ridge, located between the main town and the rebel defense line, provided lodging for the duration. Over five hundred caves, known locally as *bomb-proofs*, were dug into the yellow clay hills of Vicksburg. Whether houses were structurally sound or not, it was deemed safer to occupy these dugouts. People did their best to make them comfortable with rugs, furniture, and pictures. They tried to time their movements and foraging with the rhythm of the cannonade, sometimes unsuccessfully. Because of the citizens' burrowing, the Union soldiers gave the town the nickname of "Prairie Dog Village." Despite the ferocity of the Union fire, fewer than a dozen civilians are known to have been killed during the siege.

As of June 22, in addition to Pemberton in Vicksburg, Grant had to be aware of Confederate forces in his rear. He stationed one division in the vicinity of the Big Black River Bridge, and another reconnoitered as far north as Mechanicsburg; both acted as covering forces. By June 10, the IX Corps was transferred to Grant's command. This corps became the nucleus of a special task force, whose mission was to prevent the Confederate troop, who were gathering forces at Canton, from interfering with the siege. Sherman was given command of this task force, and another general replaced him at XV Corps. The Confederate troop eventually began moving to relieve Pemberton and reached the Big Black River on July 1, but he delayed a potentially difficult encounter with Sherman until it was too late for the Vicksburg garrison, and then fell back to Jackson. Sherman would pursue the Confederates to recapture Jackson on July 17, 1863.

On July 3, however, Pemberton sent a note to Grant regarding the possibility of negotiations for peace. Grant at first demanded unconditional surrender. He then reconsidered, not wanting to feed thirty thousand Confederates in Union prison camps, and offered to parole all prisoners. Considering their destitute and starving state, he never expected them to fight again; he hoped they would carry home the stigma of defeat to the rest of the Confederacy. In any event, shipping that many prisoners north would have occupied his army and taken months. Pemberton officially surrendered his army on July 4. Most of the men who were paroled on July 6 were exchanged and received back into the Confederate Army. Many of these soldiers did fight again and some even against Sherman's invasion of Georgia in May 1864.

Part 4

The End?

Chapter 24

During the attacks on the city, the wounded men of Michael and Jonathan's units were brought back to the Johnson Plantation for medical attention. After the first day of fighting, injured men from many units were brought back to the plantation. There were Army doctors, surgeons, and other medical personnel that took over the inactive kitchen for their surgeries. The officers had to give up four of the bedrooms and double or triple up as they were now using them for the wounded. The ballroom was set up with beds from the slave cabins and held most of the men that would be able to return to duty within a few days. Soon, the plantation looked more like a hospital than a home.

This created so much activity in the home that sometimes it was totally unclear just who was in charge and what was happening. All the Johnson women helped with the wounded, and Little Marcus became the errand boy fetching needed supplies. Although the slaves needed to maintain the crops, they too would help with the wounded when they could. Most of the neighbors would not help; this was the enemy. Bella and her family just looked at them as people and would not refuse to help them.

About three weeks after the fighting started, both Jonathan and Michael were injured. One of the injuries was not serious and one was, but Bella did not know that when she heard the news. She stopped what she was doing and ran to the surgery kitchen. Her pulse had quickened, her chest hurt, and she felt a little dizzy. First, she saw Jonathan and immediately went to check on him. He had an injury to his upper chest on the right side. It was shrapnel from a grenade. Jonathan assured her the doctor said that he could be fixed right up and back in action within a couple of days. Bella had mixed feelings about this. She was beyond thankful he would be fine but did not like hearing about him going back into battle.

Then he asked Bella to check on Michael as his wound appeared more serious. She felt panic worse than before she entered the kitchen. She searched for Michael for several minutes and then realized he was the one on the surgical table. Bella approached him and saw they were working on his left leg. She spoke to Michael, caressing his face and telling him she was there. He smiled up at her then winced at some pain. Bella looked for a bowl of water and a cloth to wash the blood off his face, neck, and hands. By talking to him about simple things, Michael seemed to relax as the surgery continued. When they finished, the doctor told him he would be fine in a couple of weeks. As they went to move him, Bella insisted they follow her. Bella led them to his room upstairs and helped get him into bed. Michael asked Bella to stop fussing over him but was very grateful she was there. He greatly enjoyed her company, and his skin tingled at her touch. She was so young, but his attraction to her was only growing stronger.

ANNABELLA'S STORY

Bella tended to him as one of the best nurses he had ever had. He had been injured before; some were minor and some not so much. This injury was somewhere in between. Bella brought him food, water, and what he enjoyed most was that she either read to him or just talked. She was so funny and her voice so enjoyable and sweet to listen to. Was he falling in love? Michael had never felt this way about any woman before. The Army had always been his mistress.

Chapter 25

About two weeks after the soldiers had arrived, Bella started noticing Union soldiers seemed to be paying too much attention to Margaret. The next day, Bella went to talk to Emma and Ellie. Mother could be more naive than most. She talked to them about what she noticed yesterday with Margaret and the soldiers. They said they had noticed it too, so they were keeping a close eye on her. As the day progressed, Bella too kept an eye on her sister. Just after dinner, Bella saw a soldier talking to Margaret. As she watched, his hand moved to her waist and slipped down. Bella immediately stopped what she was doing, and the way she quickly walked across the room left several people staring. Bella slapped the soldier across the face.

Bella placed her hands on her hips, more shouting than talking, "What do you think you are doing?"

The soldier replied, "Ouch, why did you do that?"

Bella said even louder, "My sister is not a plaything, and your hand DOES NOT belong where I saw it. Get out of this house."

The soldier smiled at Bella, saying, "Margaret doesn't seem to mind, and what are you going to do about it?"

Bella picked up a cane leaning against the wall. She swung it as hard as she could, saying, "I will hit you over and over again until you get the hell out of this house. If you ever even talk to my sister again, you will find our mastiff Bandit in your tent. DO YOU UNDERSTAND ME?" Bella kept swinging until he finally retreated.

This interaction had everyone on the first floor quiet and staring. Margaret looked at Bella, started crying, and ran to her room.

An officer nearby came over to Bella saying, "Ms. Johnson, I am so sorry. His behavior is totally unacceptable. I will resolve this." He walked out after the soldier.

Before the day ended, Colonel O'Malley had talked to Bella, her mother, and Margaret. He could not stop apologizing. He did tell them that Jonathan was responsible for the soldier's punishment. Bella knew that soldier would never talk to any of the Johnson ladies again.

A few weeks later, Colonel O'Malley was informed by Major Johnson that the fighting had stopped and a siege was taking place in Vicksburg. Unlike Jonathan, Michael had been part of a siege in prior battles and prior to this war. It was a military technique that was a last resort when the opponent's position was well fortified. Sieges could be savage on the inhabitants depending on how much food and water they had and if they could handle the sanitary conditions. Lack of sanitary conditions was usually what drove the opponent to surrender. He hated that aspect as opponents were still people and he had inspected a surrender location after they had abandoned it. Entering, it was difficult not to vomit—the smell, the human feces, the dead they couldn't bury, and the look of the people as they left their refuse. They were thin and dirty; their eyes showed so much sadness and defeat, all of which he did not share with Bella.

When Bella heard what was happening in Vicksburg, her heart ached. There were so many people that lived there whom she knew. She found herself crying the longer it went on. It was likely her father and brother were in that city. Three days later, Bella saw two soldiers talking to Marcus on the front porch. She quietly walked closer to hear the conversation as Marcus seemed very upset.

The first soldier said, "So you know your daddy is up there in Vicksburg and he's going to starve to death."

Then the second soldier chimed in, "Yeah, there are cannonballs hitting every building up there. Maybe he will be mashed by one."

Marcus started to cry, saying, "No, NO, you are lying."

Bella had been carrying some cleaned surgical knives when she heard this conversion taking place. She grabbed one of them and dropped the tray. She ran to the first soldier and slashed the arm that was on Marcus's shoulder. He pulled back, and she went after the second soldier. She cut him too and stood between Marcus and the soldiers, pointing the knife at both of them. "How dare you talk like that to a little boy? If you don't run away as fast as you can, there *will* be more cuts."

The two soldiers backed up quickly, holding their arms. They jogged over to the surgical kitchen to get stitched. Bella turned, bent down, and hugged Marcus. She whispered, "They are wrong. Your father and brother will be fine. Let's go see what sweets Emma has to eat." Marcus nodded, and the two walked into the kitchen prep area.

Later that day, O'Malley held a meeting with his officers in the dining room. About five minutes into the meeting, the doors swung open and Bella marched in.

"What kind of deviants are among you blue bellies?" Bella screamed at the top of her lungs. "First, one of your grimy soldiers put his hands on my fifteen-year-old sister, and now two old grumpy farts told Marcus his father was going to starve to death in Vicksburg. Fix this *now*, or I will instruct Emma to start poisoning your food. *Am I making myself clear?*" Her hands were in fists, and she was shaking, and the rest of the room was so silent you could hear a pin drop. Ten to fifteen seconds passed with no one speaking or moving.

Finally, Michael rose, placing his hands on the table. "Bella, you are right. There is no excuse for such behavior. The men have been away from home far too long and have definitely picked up very bad habits. What can I do to make amends?"

Jonathan also rose and moved toward Bella. "Sister, please let me assure you nothing like this will ever happen again." When he reached Bella, she fell into his arms bawling. He walked her out of the room and into the music room. Then he went and made a cup of tea for her and placed a little whiskey in it. Jonathan got her to drink it and had Ellie take her upstairs to bed. Michael and Jonathan made sure the word spread that repeated incidents like today would find the culprit hung upside down naked for no less than three days.

Chapter 26

Michael was just about healed, and soon he would have to leave. His unit was directed to move deeper into the South with General Sherman. He had made up with Bella about a week after she stormed the meeting. Michael cared so much about her and wished he could tell her. If he wanted her to know how he felt, he needed to do it soon.

General Sherman was known to destroy and burn everything in his path. He was headed to Atlanta, Georgia. Like Sherman, the South also started burning and destroying railroads or anything else the North could use against them as they retreated. However, none of the Union soldiers would try to destroy any of the buildings on the Johnson Plantation. The Johnsons had been especially kind to all the soldiers except for those two incidents with Bella standing up for her siblings. Secondly, several of the severely wounded soldiers, and one of the doctors would be staying on until they were able to leave on their own.

In total, Colonel O'Malley's forces had been on the plantation for a total of almost six weeks. There were still the five dairy cows and twenty-five goats they had started with, but they were down to twelve cows, fifteen chickens, nine sheep, and four hogs. Jonathan managed to have all seven horses remain despite the strong requests from the cavalry units. The rest had been eaten by the soldiers. Much of their reserve produce had been consumed and the crops were growing but wouldn't be ready for another four weeks. There was about a three-week supply of produce in the cold storage shed. The men had hunted as they said they would and fished when possible but even more so during the last three weeks as they were doing little fighting. This had helped slow down the consumption of the plantation reserves but wouldn't help much when they left. There would still be about thirty wounded soldiers needing to eat. Bella had requested that five to six able men and a couple of nurses be left behind to tend to the patients, move them when needed, and hunt. However, only four additional men were left with the doctor.

This was not Bella's biggest issue, what or how was she going to handle Michael leaving. She knew she was in love with him; he was all she could think about. They had never kissed, but she wanted to, and the last few nights, she cried herself to sleep. Bella thought he cared for her too, but was he in love with her? There was only one day left before they would be marching off. Bella wanted to tell Michael how she felt, but that was totally inappropriate for a Southern lady. Maybe if she could get him to take a walk and he would kiss her, maybe…

To put her plan into action, Bella started like this. "Michael, how are you feeling today?"

He had long since stopped needing her nursing, and she missed tending to him. He was walking with barely a limb but still had a little trouble mounting a horse on his own.

Bella continued, "I will be walking around the property today, inspecting and enjoying the fresh air and warmth of the sunshine. Would you like to join me?" He looked at her. Her face was lowered; he knew she didn't want him to leave. Well, he didn't want to leave her either, but the war was not over, and he was a soldier. He lifted her head, using his fingers to raise it. They gazed into each other's eyes, and he pleasantly agreed with a smile.

Bella said she would meet him in thirty minutes on the back porch. She ran to her room, touched up her hair, pinched her cheeks to give them a little color, and took a couple of deep breaths. She looked in the mirror, went to tell her mother she was going for a walk around the property, and walked as fast as she could without looking like she was walking fast to the back porch. Emma noticed as did Ellie when they saw the two together. They both did a little smile and chuckle. How could two people not know how much they loved each other? White people, they could be pretty silly sometimes.

The pair walked for about ten minutes before Bella tripped as she was not really paying much attention to the ground. Michael caught her and held on until she stood up straight. He started to walk again but did not release her hand. Bella hesitated, started to walk and didn't let go either. This was nice. Michael caressed her hand with his thumb, and Bella thought she would go insane. They chatted and walked for about another thirty minutes and found themselves in the Japanese garden with no one else around. Michael stopped and faced Bella. He paused; he couldn't remember the last time he was this nervous. Being in battle was easier than this. He finally started to talk.

Michael said, "Young lady, I have been attracted to you since the moment I saw you. Your bravery, your strength, your intelligence, and your will to fight through any obstacle."

Bella's eyes started to well up, and she responded, "I feel the same. I do not want you to leave. I know you must leave, but I do not want you to."

"You are so beautiful and I so love those eyes.

Bella said, "Yes, they look just like yours."

Michael bent down to kiss her—gently and softly. Her lips were moist and sweet, and she responded by kissing him back. He pulled back and ached for her. She was still so young. What was he to do?

Michael told her they would talk later and asked if Bella would be good to walk back to the house on her own; he needed to check on his men. He quickly walked off, and Bella wondered what was going on. Was he mad at her, or was it something she did? Bella slowly walked back to the house and decided it was time to talk to her mother as she herself knew little about men. Mother was playing the piano as she approached. Mother said she would be pleased to talk to her daughter, not sure of the topic but confident she would try to help her daughter with that man.

Mother and Bella walked to her bedroom arm and arm. Mother sat down on her bed and instructed Bella to pull over a chair. Bella stumbled and mumbled nonsense for a few minutes. Mother grabbed her hand, patted it with the other, and smiled at her daughter saying, "You are attracted to that Colonel O'Malley."

Bella lowered her head and eyes. "Mother, how did you know?"

Mother said, "You look at him like I looked at your father. And he looks at you like your father looked at me when we first met."

"Mother, what do I do? We just took a walk. He told me he cared about me and did not want to leave but that he must. He then kissed me." Bella paused, remembering that kiss. "But I don't understand what he did next. He pulled away, said that we would talk later and he needed to check on his men. Mother, did I do something wrong, or did I forget to do something? Please help me."

Mother said, "You have done nothing wrong my daughter," smiling softly. "He is a little older than you and correctly assumes you are inexperienced with men. He is a soldier, and his duty is to lead his men until the war is over. I may not understand this war, but I do understand how an officer will behave."

As Bella watched her mother speak, she continued, "Darling, wish him safe journeys. Kiss his cheek and tell him you will wait if he means that much to you...but if you are not sure, let him leave without a word."

"Mother, I love him," Bella said as she cried.

Mother said, "Bella, go to your room. I will have Emma bring you up some tea. Read your Bible, and you will decide what is best."

Bella did as instructed and spent a few hours reading and drinking tea. By teatime, she knew what she would do. Tomorrow they were leaving, so Bella sent a message to her brother to be sure to stop by in the morning before leaving.

The next morning, Bella rose at six o'clock as usual, dressed, and descended to the dining room. As she walked into the kitchen prep room, she saw Emma and Ellie talking, whispering actually. She then said, "What's going on? Has something happened?"

Emma looked at her with sad eyes. "Ms. Bella, the soldiers be gone. Th'y leav' 'bout thirty minutes ago. Mr. Jonath'n say to tell you they be back wh'n they can and he luv 'u." Bella wasn't sure what to do; she just stood there silent and still.

Then she just ran. Bella was out the front door, across to the stables, and pulled Sugar out of her stall. She used a stool to mount her bareback and took off at a gallop. It took no time at all to see the rear of the Army. She continued past them to the front. As she got closer, the men started shouting. Bella was unaware of what they were saying, but whatever it was, the officers up front stopped and looked behind them.

Both Jonathan and Michael moved their mounts over to the side of the road and waited. Bella pulled up short, gasping for breath. She looked at Jonathan then at Michael. "Why did you leave without saying goodbye? I thought you cared about me. You just left…so what am I to think? I love you." Bella's eyes welled with tears.

Michael's mouth opened, but no words came out. He dismounted his horse, walked over to Bella, and pulled her off Sugar and into his embrace. He then kissed her—gently at first then a deep meaningful kiss. Together they embraced for what seemed like hours to Bella. Finally, he pulled back and looked at her. "I love you too, my little sunshine," Michael said without hesitation.

Bella said, "I will wait for you. Fight well, and return to me. Now go, lead your men, and keep my brother safe. I want you both back." She then looked at Jonathan. "How dare you leave without saying goodbye? If you and Michael do not return, I will find you and drag you back." Then Bella smiled. "Now get down here, and help me back on my horse. I have work to do."

Jonathan did as instructed, but hugged his sister and gave her a kiss on the top of her head before he did. As he led her horse back in the direction in which she came, he said, "You are such a strong young lady. Keep up the good work." Then he whacked Sugar on the rump, and off she went.

Chapter 27

It was approximately ten days after the Union Army left that the City of Vicksburg surrendered. It was July 4, 1863. Word came that the soldiers were being paroled and the civilians were able to get badly needed food, water, and medicine. General Grant thought the Confederates would return to their homes defeated, but he was wrong.

Father and Andrew led seven hundred of the close to thirty thousand paroled troops toward the plantation. There he knew he and his men could recover and return to the fight. They had to stop General Sherman before he burned the entire South to ash. It took two days to reach the plantation as the men were weak, but eventually, they arrived. Emanuel was the first to see the soldiers; they wore tattered clothes and were thin and approaching very slowly. He ran to the house and yelled for Bella. Then he saw the Union soldiers in the ballroom, and a panic ran through him. What would happen when they saw each other? Oh, one thing at a time.

ANNABELLA'S STORY

When Emanuel found Bella, he told her who was approaching. She looked excited and started to move when Emanuel grabbed her arm. "Ms. Bella, sorry, but look, th'r be Union soldiers in th'r. What we go'ng to do?"

Bella stopped in her tracks. *Oh my, this is not going to be good*, she thought. When she reached her father, she hugged him and hugged him and hugged him. Then Andrew joined them, and they all hugged. After a few moments, Bella started, "Father, I must talk to you before you reach the house."

Meanwhile, inside the house, the soldiers that stayed behind spotted the Confederates approaching. There was some panic. Those able, all grabbed muskets and went to the windows. The sergeant in charge said to wait until Ms. Bella returned; he hoped she could keep everyone safe with some sort of truce.

Father looked at Bella with some concern, saying, "What is it, Bella? Is someone hurt, sick, what?"

Bella hesitantly replied, "Father, Jonathan and many of the Union soldiers were here during the siege of the City. They have left, but there are still some that were seriously injured, a doctor and a few able bodied others to help and do hunting. Father, can we have peace until they are able to leave. Let's not fight here, not on the Plantation, not in our house."

Father looked at Andrew, and together they stood there staring until Andrew started to speak. "Father, you know what we just went through, we cannot let them live." The anger in his voice scared Bella.

Father said as he looked at his son, "How could I forget? Bloodshed in our home, no. This war has already taken such a toll on both sides. I understand your anger, but I want to think for a few minutes."

Father, Andrew, and Bella all stood quiet for several minutes. Meanwhile, both troops were getting a little restless, unsure of what was happening. The Southern soldiers were all tired, hungry and irritable. Finally, Father spoke again. "Bella, take me inside alone, and I will talk to whoever is in charge. Andrew, you and the men stay here, and I will return shortly."

Father and Bella turned and walked to the house. As they walked, Father wanted to know where Edwin was. She explained about the attack and death of Marie and then what happened after. Father shook his head, one more thing that just shouldn't have happened—his little girl having to run a plantation and manage all the needed duties. They were met just inside the front door by two Union soldiers plus the sergeant and the doctor. The soldiers had muskets; however, they were at their sides and not pointed. Father spoke first. "My name is Colonel John Johnson. This is my family home. May we talk about how we can best handle this situation of both sides being here together?"

The doctor and sergeant looked at each other and nodded. The sergeant told his men to stay calm and to stand guard, but no one was to do anything without his permission.

All three men walked into the dining room to discuss options.

The Union sergeant started with "Sir, most of these men were seriously wounded. That is why we are still here. We are in no position to attack or to defend ourselves."

John looked at the sergeant, and then the doctor said, "We do not need any more bloodshed right now, especially to wounded men. How many of you are there?"

"We have thirty wounded, this doctor here, and three other soldiers beside myself," said the sergeant in response.

"It would be better if the men were on different floors and to limit their contact with each other. Can you move all the wounded upstairs into the various rooms? Then we can keep everyone apart easier," explained John.

Then it was the doctor's turn. "Yes, we could, but it would take time with only the five of us to move them."

John rose concluding with "I will select the right men to come and help. Be sure your men know we must all stay calm to stay safe."

The sergeant stood and shook John's hand, saying, "Sir, we will. Thank you. We will start moving the wounded now."

The sergeant talked to his men, and with the doctor's help, the wounded were starting to move upstairs.

ANNABELLA'S STORY

John returned to his men and talked to Andrew, who was not pleased but did as ordered. John selected five men, told them what he needed, and they moved off toward the house. He then instructed Andrew to start setting up some of the men in the barn, in the schoolhouse, and every other building where people could rest out of the sun. Those needing immediate medical attention were taken to the house. Although there were two doctors among the eight hundred men, the Union doctor offered to help if needed. Doctors didn't seem to care about sides, just helping people.

Bella talked to her mother, Emma, and Ellie about what was happening. The women started on a plan to feed the new arrivals. Emma knew from past experience with undernourished slaves that they needed to intake food slowly and to keep the food light such as broths, soups, and breads. The slave women started preparing food.

They put all the Union soldiers in the four bedrooms along the left side of the second floor. It was somewhat cramped, but everyone fit. The doctor stayed in the small sitting room in the back and one soldier slept outside each of the bedroom doors. The sergeant slept closest to the stairs in case there were any incidents to address. The Johnson family continued to sleep upstairs with Father and Mother and Marcus in the master bedroom, the three girls in the medium room, and two even-tempered Confederate officers in the front bedroom. Andrew stayed in various buildings with the men. Father and he thought it best not to have him that close to the Northern soldiers.

The more seriously sick or injured Southern soldiers now occupied the ballroom. However, the mood and atmosphere was tense for the first week. Emma and Ellie, with Mimi's help, had to work hard to keep food prepared for all the men. By the end of the week, several were able to start helping with acquiring food through hunting and fishing. The Union soldiers stayed in the house as instructed by Confederate Colonel Johnson. These men were surprised that this rebel colonel was so generous considering the circumstances and this being his home.

Andrew did take a few meals with his family, but the family was sure to let the Union people know, so they stayed upstairs. After the first meal they shared, Marcus wanted to talk to Andrew about his missing hand. Andrew had decided that when he did not need to use it directly, it was better to put a leather glove over the hook and tuck it under his sleeve. This way, he could still use it to hold and move things but would not accidentally hurt anyone if they bumped into him. Andrew had it specially made so there were no loose glove fingers hanging down and some padding inside the glove to fill it out.

Andrew did not go into great detail as he did not want to scare Marcus about why and how his hand was gone. He just told him his hand was injured and needed to be taken off. He went ahead and took off his glove and removed his hook. Marcus watched but felt a mixture of fright and fascination. Andrew removed the cloth that covered the skin to reduce the irritation while wearing his hook. He then told Marcus if he wanted, he could touch it. Marcus hesitated but reached out to touch Andrew's remaining skin. Marcus was surprised about how it felt and was now calmer about the hook. Marcus also handled the hook while it was off but Andrew asked him to be careful; it was sharp. Andrew put everything back on including his glove. Now that Marcus's curiosity was satisfied, the two brothers talked of other things and laughed.

The next day, Bella gave her boxes of letters to both Father and Andrew. Then she realized that Mother, Margaret, and Lizzie all came down with boxes of letters. Marcus brought down pictures of birds he drew for his father and brother. Everyone was surprised. No one knew the others were keeping these items. Father and Andrew were very touched and each let a tear roll down their cheeks. Later that night, they each found a quiet place to sit and read the letters. This caused both of them to smile, laugh, be sad, and even shed tears. It wasn't until then that they both realized how much they had missed their family and for Andrew how much he had changed. He did *not* like how he felt but there was no turning back now…

About eight days after the confederate soldiers arrived, it finally happened. Two of the northern soldiers were on the front porch getting some fresh air. Three southern soldiers exited the same door and saw them there. Next, there were a few moments of silence and then shouting, name calling, and eventually some pushing. The sergeant, the doctor, and Andrew all heard the noise and went running toward it. As they all came to the porch, the tension became more intense.

Andrew started in a firm and angry voice, "You blue bellies need to keep the hell away from us. I am not my father, and I have no problem killing you all. You have no right to be in the South and especially in this house. You have five seconds to get back upstairs or find yourself dead."

The doctor replied in his calmest voice, "Sir, we are sorry. We will leave here as soon as possible."

All the while, he and the sergeant were pulling the Union soldiers inside. Both of them knew it would likely get worse very soon if they didn't stop it now. Colonel John heard about the incident; he also knew it was likely things would escalate into something he did not want. His family was here, his wife and daughters. He needed a solution. John decided to talk to the doctor about the progress of his patients. The doctor said that they could leave in about ten days if they could wait until then; that's when most of the men would be able to walk on their own.

John placed two of his more sensible officers to stay close to the Union soldiers in addition to the two sleeping upstairs. He warned the sergeant to keep a close watch on his men then discussed how to plan their departure without incident. There were no further issues in the ongoing days. Finally, the day came for the Union soldiers to leave. The only ones aware of the plan were the sergeant and John—the fewer, the better. John planned a large meal gathering for all his men around 8:00 p.m. It would be held out by the barn in one of the open fields. He had some of the men build a bonfire and had some special foods prepared by Emma for the occasion. This would distract the soldiers and get them away from the house.

At 7:30 p.m., the sergeant told his men to gather up their things; they were leaving in fifteen minutes. Quietly, the group exited by the front door and walked quietly toward the road. They then continued north toward Vicksburg to join up with their fellow soldiers. They did take five muskets with them, ammunition, and some food and water. All proceeded as planned until about 8:30 p.m.

Most of the Union wounded in the ballroom were unable to attend the gathering by the barn. A few were still not well enough, and their doctor had been told by John to keep the doors closed so the departure by the North would not be noticed. Regardless of side, doctors did not want to see more men killed. Shortly before 8:00 p.m., one of the Union soldiers went to check on his wounded friend. As he entered the house, he thought something seemed different. He sat down beside his friend, and they started talking. The wounded soldier told the first man that he thought he heard a lot of movement a short time ago and then there was silence. He thought the rebels had left. The first soldier checked and found they were all gone.

This soldier then proceeded to Andrew to inform him as he too was not happy they were allowed to live. Andrew discreetly gathered a few men and their muskets and started after the group. As the Confederate soldiers were in better condition, they overtook the Union troops within a short period. Shooting erupted. By the time it was over, most of the Union troops were either dead or wounded, and only two of the Confederates were wounded. Andrew had the Union wounded killed and all the bodies dragged off the road and out of sight. The revenge he felt was strong, and he would make them paid as much as he could.

Unbeknownst to his father, Andrew had organized a few scouting parties in the last couple of weeks to identify where Union soldiers remained near Vicksburg. He knew they may not be able to take the city back, but that didn't mean he couldn't still do some damage. This small unit led by Andrew hit in a variety of places quickly and quietly so as not to arouse suspicion. He knew these actions would be irritating to the Union but probably wouldn't lead them to finding them as they were sure to attack in several different areas away from the plantation. Upon their return that night, Andrew saw to his wounded men and reminded the small group that discretion was essential or his father may court-martial them all.

ANNABELLA'S STORY

Andrew was very bitter. His childhood home was in the middle of Northern troops. The prospects of the South ultimately losing were great, and he did not want to accept defeat. He would fight to the end, and…so would his men. A week later, John's group of soldiers were ready to go back into battle. They needed to find guns and ammo, so they had sent out scouts and found a general to join up with. They would be leaving within the next few days to fight the Union soldiers again.

The departure of Father and Andrew was a very tearful event. Unlike when Jonathan left, it was thought but unsaid that it was less likely for Father and Andrew to return than Jonathan. As much food as possible was sent with the men, and huge hugs and kisses were given by the family members. That night, Bella cried into her pillow, and she could hear her mother doing the same.

Chapter 28

During the rest of 1863 and most of 1864, the days moved slowly but the months even slower. Activities had returned to what was now normal. The plantation would get word now and then about what was happening in the war. There was Sherman's March to the Sea during the end of 1864. General Sherman marched through Georgia and destroyed much of the South's infrastructure including telegraphs, railroads, and bridges. As he had done elsewhere, every plantation in his path was severely damaged, leaving much of the South in ruins.

The Johnson Plantation buildings stayed intact, but there were often Union troops "stopping" by. They would take whatever they wanted—livestock, chickens, eggs, produce, and feed for their horses. They were able to keep Blaze and Daisy, the black Shire horses, hidden, but the Northerners were able to take Dakota and Sadie, the Irish draft horses. Bella did her best to stop the soldiers from taking them but to no avail.

President Lincoln declared all slaves free with the Emancipation Proclamation on January 1, 1863. Like when O'Malley and Jonathan were on the plantation, each time Union troops came by, they told the slaves on the plantation. They always responded by saying they were not slaves but freely worked there in exchange for food and shelter. President Abraham Lincoln was reelected in 1864, but on April 14, 1865, he was assassinated.

The next news the Johnsons received was that Confederate General Robert E. Lee surrendered to General Ulysses S. Grant on April 9, 1865. Next, General Joseph E. Johnston surrendered to

ANNABELLA'S STORY

General William T. Sherman on April 26, 1865. Although Bella feared as it appeared the Confederacy was going to lose, it also meant the war may be ending soon. What would happen then?

As Bella did not know where any of her family were fighting, all the news received made her worry more. Father and Andrew were with General Johnston when he surrendered to Sherman. During the fighting, many lives were lost. Andrew and his men got trapped, and refusing to surrender, they all perished. Father was also injured, and it was unclear if he would lose his left foot. Meanwhile, O'Malley and Jonathan were on the opposing side. Neither of them were seriously injured and never knew their family was there. Skirmishes and battles continued for the next few months, but the war was considered over.

Bella and her family started to see Northern troops leave and a few Southern troops return. Where was her family? Days, then weeks, then two months later, Father rode up to the plantation drive in a wagon full of war-torn soldiers. One of the other soldiers got down before Father to help him off the wagon and escorted him to the house. Bella called her mother and siblings. As Father approached, they noticed he had a crutch. The family ran to him, yelling and screaming shoots of joy. When they met, Mother hugged him so hard they almost fell to the ground. She pulled back and looked him up then down. Next, she gasped; Father's left foot was missing.

"Oh my darling, are you well? What has happened to you?" Mother said through her tears.

Father said, "I will be fine. This is Hamilton. He will be staying with us for a while." He pointed to the man helping him. Father continued, "He has an idea on how to get me walking on my own again." Father then leaned forward with Hamilton's assistance to hug each of his children individually. He was so thankful to be home and see all of them again. There were several times he had been sure he would never return.

Hamilton Franklin had been one of Father's first lieutenants and had kept him organized. He also took care of his correspondence, shining his boots, helping him dress, and tending to his horse among other duties. He was a short man at 5'9" but broad and muscular. He had blond-brown hair with pale-brown eyes. Father had started using Hamilton's talents after leaving the Plantation and the loss at Vicksburg. He had no family of his own and was especially loyal to John. If not for Hamilton, the colonel would have died in their last battle.

Everyone headed to the house and gathered in the front parlor. Ellie brought glasses of lemonades for everyone and a plate of cheeses and breads to eat. Emma, Big George, and Raymond all came to the door of the parlor. "Welcome home, Mr. John," they all said one at a time.

"Thank you," Father replied, and the three left along with Ellie.

Chatting continued with everyone so excited. Finally, Bella paused. "Father, where is Andrew? Why is he not with you?"

Father hung his head, and his eyes welled up with tears. He raised his head, saying nothing. His silence became an ominous quiet. Then Mother started screaming, "No, no, no. Please tell me he is not… Please, John, let it not be so."

Father slowly nodded, and then all the sisters knew he had been killed. Marcus was ten years old at this time and wasn't exactly sure what was happening. Bella reached for him to explain that Andrew would never be coming home; he had died.

Chapter 29

The next week, everyone tried to settle into a new routine. Father stayed in one of the empty bedrooms on the left side of the second floor, and a cot was set up for Hamilton in the same room. Father wanted to do this until he could move around better. Hamilton was helping him get from here to there, and Father did not want to distress his wife any more than she already was. He was still a little weak from the injury plus the journey home. Emma's good cooking and medical herbs would fix him right up. Bella had moved back to the front bedroom on the right shortly after Father, Andrew, and all the southern soldiers had left almost two years ago. Lizzie and Margaret stayed in the middle room, and Marcus moved back into the small room across from Mother.

Bella continued her routines she had taken over after Uncle Edwin died but began turning things back over to Father. She continued the daily inspections as Father could not ride. Then she would report everything back to him and what she and Big George had decided needed to be done that day. If Father wanted to change anything, Bella would relay that information to Big George. John was very impressed with how his daughter had run the plantation. He doubted he could have done much better himself under the circumstances.

Hamilton had used the blacksmith house to design a metal apparatus for John. He cut and made straps with buckles to attach to John's leg. They placed a soft cloth next to his skin to reduce any irritation from the metal. Then they worked on John learning to walk again. Eventually, he accomplished it for the most part but would always need a cane, and some assistance in mounting a horse but could easily ride once on one.

As Father became healthy and more relaxed, he needed to address how to run a plantation without slaves. He decided to try a few methods as now all the former slaves still needed to earn a living. He paid the slaves that had stayed a good wage and others a lesser amount who came to work for him. He also took on several sharecroppers in the outer fields. And like several other plantation owners, he did use some contracts to gain workers. The contracts, in reality, were similar to slavery. This pretty much trapped the Negros into working forever as they were unlikely to ever get ahead financially.

Within six months, John had three hundred workers for the fields. They would start planting in a few months. Before then, work was needed on several buildings, fixing equipment, and repairing the slave cabins. Although now they would be called worker cabins. Workers could either pay rent or receive a lower wage, whichever they preferred. These processes were new to everyone and took a few years to get the flow to become normal.

The new workers were immediately able to open the other two greenhouses and started preparing the remaining tobacco for shipping. The previously unused fields also needed to be cleared of overgrowth and debris. This material would all be burned.

To bring in dollars until the next crop, Father sold the rest of the tobacco and some of the extra produce and crops that had built up in storage. Although he truly hated it, Father also had to sell Blaze and Daisy. The pair were sold at a great price, but Mother had cried after. John promised her they would get another pair when the plantation got back on its feet. He replaced them with cheaper workhorses and could purchase four good horses and still have money left over. They would still need horses to plow the fields and pull wagons.

Chapter 30

One year had passed since Father's return, and things were returning to the way it was prior to the war with a few changes. The slaves were no longer slaves but paid workers. Grandmother and Grandfather Morgan had returned from England and took up residence in the same house as before. They brought back with them some new pieces of furniture for their home and other items to give to their grandchildren. Crops, especially cotton, were back to being a money making crop. As promised, Father bought a new pair of Shire Draft horses. The pair were just as beautiful as Blaze and Daisy. They stood slightly taller and were given the names of Pepper and Athena. Together the first new foal was born on the plantation in over five years.

There was still no sign of Johnathan or Michael. Were they dead? Would they ever return? Many nights, Bella would cry herself to sleep. And on some nights, she could hear others crying as well. Bella was now twenty-one years old, and her parents were talking to her about getting married. There were a few appropriate men, officers that had returned from the war, who would make a good husband. Bella realized sooner or later, she would have to give in. She prayed that Michael would return before it was too late.

It was about a week after Bella turned twenty-one that a man rode down the drive toward the house. He was on a beautiful gray quarter horse. He wore good commoner clothes in greens and browns and a wide-brimmed tan man's hat. He knocked on the door and waited. Raymond answered the door then stood back and stared. Before him stood Mr. Andrew. He had a long scar down the right side of his face mostly hidden with a thick beard, but otherwise he seemed healthy. Andrew spoke, "Hello, Raymond. It's been a long time. Is my father here?" Raymond stepped back and led Andrew into the library where his father was working.

John turned from his desk as the door opened. When he saw Andrew, he almost fell out of his chair trying to get up. Andrew walked quickly to his father and steadied him, and they embraced. "Oh, thank the Lord you are alive. My son, where have you been?" said Father as he wiped a tear from his cheek.

Andrew said, "It is a very long story. I am just so happy you made it home, Father. Let's find Mother and the rest of the family." The pair walked into the hallway looking for their family. Meanwhile, Raymond had already gathered them up, and everyone ended up meeting in front of the library. Everyone was hugging, yelling, and laughing with joy. Raymond, Emma, Ellie, and Mimi watched from down the hall. They too were very happy Andrew was home. Now if only Jonathan would return.

It was close to dinnertime, so the family was very festive as they enjoyed their meal. Later, Andrew met with his father again in the library to talk of what he had been doing and what he had been through. Andrew began, "When we were surrounded, myself and two others were able to get out and around to flank the blue bellies. But before we could do much, the men had all been shot and were dead. The three of us still fought with those savages. We were all injured, but these men wanted to do more than just kill us. The 'soldiers' did not take us back to their camp—they took us to a clearing close by. There, they tortured my men, and I was made to watch. They cut them with blades and hit them over and over again." Without knowing, Andrew's eyes had started to well up.

A few moments later, he lifted his head with sheer hatred visible and continued. "They beat them for about thirty minutes before the pair died. Then another group of blue bellies must have heard the commotion and came running. There was a sergeant with them, and he made them stop. He said they would be shot for their behavior, but I doubted it would ever happen. Before the others could grab them, one of the torturers slashed my face." He pointed to the scar.

ANNABELLA'S STORY

"Then I was sent to a prison for almost six months. Conditions were far worse than they were at the end of the Vicksburg siege. There we had little food, no clean water, no medical attention, and hostile guards."

Andrew rose from his chair and went over to the liquor cabinet. He poured himself a glass of bourbon and gestured to his father if he wanted one. Father nodded. Andrew poured a second glass and brought them back to where they had been sitting. Andrew continued his story. "Everyone was released due to the 'end' of the war. Five of the men I grew to know walked out with me, and we found a friendly home. These true Southerners fed us, cleaned us up, and tended to our injuries and lack of nutrition. We stayed a couple of weeks until we were close to being healthy and strong. They were able to give us a couple of guns, and we left. Together we have been fighting on and returning their savage behavior. If it is all right with you, Father, I would like to have these men stay here."

Father was concerned about the last part of Andrew's story. Had his son become an outlaw or vigilante or something? He did agree to let the men stay but asked Andrew to caution them about being mindful of the children, his sisters in particular, and the sanctity of their home. Andrew kind of glared at his father and nodded but said nothing.

Andrew said he would be back shortly; he was going to let his men know to come to the Plantation. He also told Father he would stop in the kitchen to let Emma know about the extra guests. Father's worry increased hearing Andrew call the others *his men*.

An hour or so later, Andrew returned with five other men. Each of them were moderately dressed, carried hand pistols, and rode good, strong-looking horses. There were also muskets on their saddles and knives in sheaves on their belts. Andrew led them to the stables, where Emanuel greeted them and took their horses to be stabled. Emanuel unsaddled the horses, and now that Noah was old enough, both he and Daniel helped brush the horses down and get them feed and water. Meanwhile, the men started back toward the house.

Andrew introduced all the men to Father, then he showed them to their rooms. The four men would need to decide who would double up. There were only three empty bedrooms as Hamilton was in one of the room on the left. Bella agreed to go back in with her sisters so Andrew could have her room. The last man, Michael, known as Mickey, had always lived a simple life and preferred to sleep in the stables with the horses.

During teatime, all the men with Andrew were introduced to the family. First, there was George Wallace, a former first lieutenant in the Confederate Army. He was 5'10" tall and about 180 pounds. He had dark-blond hair and pale-blue eyes. Andrew left out other details about each man. For George, he had become very skilled with a knife, was twenty-five years old, and his entire family had been killed during war. Next, Norman Cross, known as Norm, was a former sergeant. He was 5'11" tall and 200 pounds. His hair was brown as were his eyes, and he was thirty years old. Unknown was that Norm was very strong and was very good at hand-to-hand fighting. His mother was still alive, but his brother had lost an arm in war.

The third man, William Smith, known as Billy or Red, was also a former soldier. He was six feet tall and 220 pounds, with bright-red hair and moss-green eyes. He was twenty-two years old. His unmentioned skills were that he was good with a knife and an accurate shot. Red had lost his father and brother in war, while his mother and one sister had moved in with his uncle. The fourth man, Simon Thomas, was a former soldier and had fought with Billy in the same unit. He was 5'8" tall and overweight at 250 pounds. He was the oldest in the group at forty-two years old with a balding head of thin brown hair and light-brown eyes. The men knew he had been whipped by Northern soldiers and his back was badly scarred. He had hunted often before the war and now was an excellent sharpshooter.

The last and final member was Michael Barkley, known as Mickey. He was a former second lieutenant, stood 5'10", and weighed about 200 pounds. Mickey was twenty-eight years old with blond/brown hair and dark-blue eyes. He was an excellent tracker and was very loyal to Andrew for Andrew had saved his life several times during battles. Mickey was also a proficient fighter with his fists, a knife, and a gun. Some of the men had beards like Andrew, including Simon, George, and Mickey. The other two, Red and Norm, were clean-shaven, but they could all use a haircut. The men were well-mannered and well-spoken except for Red; his grammar was a little rough.

The conversation during teatime was casual and easy with no one bringing up any mention of the war. Around 9:00 p.m., everyone but the men left the parlor for bed. The men continued in conversation and drinking bourbon, talking of some of the events of the war as they were all former soldiers. It was close to midnight when the men broke up and retired to their sleeping quarters.

The next morning, Andrew and the men were up early, and Emma agreed to go ahead and fix them some breakfast. They were very thankful and told Emma so. Then they retrieved their horses and rode off into Vicksburg. There the men split up and wandered the city. They were seeing where any remaining Union soldiers were stationed and if they could identify any carpetbaggers. The latter was the name given to a Northerner who went to the South after the Civil War for political or financial advantage. They also searched for any target in which they would have financial gain to support them on their travels.

Each pair walked around for about two hours before heading back to the plantation. They didn't want to all be seen together; it would draw too much attention to them. They met up just outside of the city and discussed what each group had found. They would harm all the Northerners and carpetbaggers either temporarily or permanently. They had learned to be discreet so they could do maximum damage before they needed to head out. There were two locations to gain funds. One was the bank, and the other the Clement Plantation. This plantation was rumored to have all their money on site. Over the next few days, they would work on eliminating the people then how to take the Clement Plantation and the bank in the same day.

One late afternoon, Marcus was on the back porch, and three of the new men were standing there talking and having a smoke: Norm, George, and Mickey. Marcus approached as he had been very curious about the knives he saw each man had.

Marcus said, "Hello, I like your knives. May I see them?"

Mickey, pulling out his Bowie knife, replied, "Sure."

As Marcus looked at it, he said in awe, "That sure is a long blade. What do you use it for?"

Mickey replied, "I am a tracker, and I use it to cut away branches in my way and defend myself if I scare a wild animal and it attacks."

As his eyes grew big, Marcus said, "Wow, has that happened?"

Mickey finished with "Yes, a couple of times. Usually, the animal just turns and runs."

Norm pulled out his knife as Mickey returned his to its sheaf. "Mine is a Hudson Bay knife. I like the wide width and eight-inch length for cutting up deer." Actually, Norm was now using it to cut up people.

George pulled his out next and knelt down closer to Marcus, "This is a Plains dagger. See how both sides are sharp and the point is also sharp. I like to use it for…throwing." George threw the knife at the nearest tree and didn't mention that it was also good for stabbing the enemy up close.

Marcus said, "Amazing, can you teach me to throw?"

Before George could answer, Bella saw the group on the back porch, noticing they were all showing Marcus their knives. So she called out, "Marcus, Mother would like to see you," just to get him away from them.

As Marcus entered the house, Bella walked over to the three men. "Please do not encourage him with your knives—he is still a little young for that. Thank you."

The men had been on site for about two weeks and knew they would be leaving soon. They couldn't stay in any one place very long. Everyone was behaving themselves, and now that they were "working," no one was allowed to have an alcoholic drink until after they left. Mimi offered to cut everyone's hair, which they all accepted. They liked the job she did, so each gave her a little money.

The next morning, the men were going out to have some target practice. Andrew required them to do it three times each week. No one minded; it was relaxing to the men and kept their aim sharp. While they were waiting for Andrew to come outside, Red said, "I like that Lizzie girl. Her hair has some red like mine. Maybe I will give her a kiss."

George said, "Well, I like the one with the brown hair—she has the most beautiful eyes. I could just sink right into them."

Billy said, "Are you two trying to get yourselves killed? Do you know what Andrew would do to you if he heard you talk about his sisters like that, let alone you actually try anything? You would definitely be missing a few body parts." The others nodded, and no mention of the sisters happened again.

Father started hearing of property damage and deaths to some in the area. They all appeared to be from the North or collaborators of the North. Father hoped this wasn't due to Andrew and his men. They were gone enough to have performed these activities. He didn't seem to know his son anymore. Father prayed for his son and that he was wrong about what these men were doing. He had inquired once on what they had been doing and what they would do next, but he didn't get a straight answer. Seeing how uncomfortable Andrew had become, Father decided not to continue along this path of conversation.

Chapter 31

Two days prior to the date Andrew and his men had decided to leave, five new men rode down the drive on horseback. As they approached the house, two of the men dismounted and headed for the door. The others dismounted and stayed with the horses. The pair stepped up on the porch, and one of the men opened the door and walked in. A familiar voice called out, "Hello, hello, is anyone home?"

"Jonathan…you're home!" Bella screamed as she ran down the stairs to the front door. "Everyone, Jonathan is home, hurry, hurry." Bella was moving so fast, she almost fell down the stairs. Everyone came running and gathered in the foyer. The only ones not present were Father and Hamilton as they were out talking to the workers at the brick making building. Raymond jogged out to let Father know Jonathan was back.

As Father walked toward the house, he inadvertently said out loud, "I hope he and Andrew will remember they are brothers." Hamilton looked at Father, and the two hurried on.

Meanwhile, Bella stepped back so others could get to Jonathan and looked out the open door. The man standing in the doorway had taken off his hat, but the sun was shining at such an angle it was hard to see his face. He took another step inside, and then she saw him: Michael—in living color. Bella ran the few steps needed to close the distance and leaped into his arms. She was laughing and crying at the same time as Michael hugged her so tight she could barely breathe.

Everyone turned and saw the pair. There were smiles on every face. Emma, Ellie, and Mimi were smiling from the dining room with tears in their eyes. Michael released Bella and bent down to give Bella a kiss. Everyone's smile just grew bigger. Then he turned to the family saying, "Hello, everyone. It's great to be back." As Michael realized that Mr. Johnson was standing in the group, he walked over to introduce himself and shake his hand. Then he continued. "Mr. Johnson, my name is Michael O'Malley, and I am in love with your daughter. I would like your permission to marry her."

Silence filled the room while Mother and Bella both raised their hands to their faces and gasped. Then Father spoke. "Well, young man, I believe that before I answer, I would like to get to know you better." There were several chuckles, including Michael.

Father knew they probably had a bigger issue to worry about before he could address what to do about Bella. He motioned Jonathan and Michael back into the library to talk, and Hamilton followed close behind. "I am so very happy to see you, my son, but your brother…well, I am not sure what he has become."

Jonathan replied, "What do you mean?"

Father continued, "He is traveling with five other former Confederate soldiers, and based on what I can tell, they are killing and robbing any Northerner they can find. Several people have died around the general area recently. When I tried to talk to him, it was clear he was not going to talk to me."

Jonathan looked at Michael, and then Michael began talking. "Sir, we have seen this before. Unfortunately, John and I have been hunting former Confederates who are not willing to move on. I understand your son is a gifted strategist. I am sure they are not going to welcome us being here. How much longer are they going to stay?"

Father thought for a few moments. "They said they would be leaving in two days. What do you want to do?"

Michael again took the lead. "First, we will need to change into non-military clothes. Be sure our uniforms are well hidden. Next, we will stay out of sight in one of the kitchen sleeping quarters. I believe those are the former slaves most loyal to you. No one else can know we are here. Will your children be able to stay quiet about us? Marcus seemed very excited that John is home, and he is still just a child. It may be hard for him not to talk." They were all quiet for another few moments.

"I will send my wife and the youngest three children to a friend's house further outside the city. They have gone there before to visit and help out. They have already got there once while Andrew has been here," said Father.

Jonathan said, "Then send them now before Andrew comes back and have Big George release the horses to the pasture so they blend in with the other horses, and we will go to the kitchen. We must hurry."

Everyone moved and put the actions into place.

Mother and the children were just leaving the drive with Emanuel steering the carriage when Andrew and his men arrived. Father was standing on the porch as the men came forward to the stables. He had instructed Bella to stay in her bedroom and not ask questions. Bella had never heard her father be so stern. She thought his voice even seemed a little scared. Father told his son that his mother and siblings were going to visit the Andersons again but would be back before they left the day after tomorrow.

Andrew said, "That is unfortunate as we will be leaving tonight."

Father responded, "What is the hurry?"

"Something has happened, and our plans have changed," Andrew said as he entered the house.

What he was not saying was that they had come up with a plan to take the monetary targets, and it was best to do it quickly and get out. They knew there were rumblings about all the recent deaths.

Father tried to sound sincere, "I am sorry you must leave so quickly. Do you want me to instruct Emma to get some food ready for you to take?"

"Thank you, Father," Andrew said. "We have all appreciated your hospitality. I am not sure when I will get back this way, but I will try not to make it too long."

All the men shook hands, said their goodbyes, and the men climbed the staircase to gather their belongings. Father found Emma and had her prepare some food for the men to take with them. She put together some smoked ham, some fresh produce, a few loaves of bread, and some coffee beans. She wrapped items in separate pieces of cloth and put them into three bags. She then gave the bags to Raymond to take out to stables and the awaiting horses.

Father also asked Emma to send Ellie to him immediately. Father then instructed Ellie to go to the kitchen Jonathan and Michael were in and let them know Andrew and his men were leaving within the hour and seemed in quite a hurry. Upon this news, Michael and Jonathan knew they needed to follow this group. It was likely these were the men they had been chasing for a while. The group was known as the Rebel 6 and had the reputation of brutal behavior to those they came across. The Rebel 6 cut throats, tortured men with knives and fireplace pokers, and slaughtered the children before they left. Sometimes they even tied the living to chairs and burned the place down. They were savages. The war definitely wasn't over for them. Michael asked Ellie to have Big George come to talk to them. By the time Big George arrived, they had a plan.

Andrew and his men left as planned and headed for Vicksburg. They would go to the hotel and share a meal, waiting for the right time to strike. Norm had spent some time wooing one of the bank tellers named Beth. She agreed to let him meet her at the bank at closing time to walk her home as he had done several times in the past. This had also gotten him close to the assistant bank manager, a small, mousy man easily intimidated named Steven. Norm usually arrived just before closing. The manager would lock the door while the last of the money was counted and put in the safe. Norm had been there several times for this process, and Steven said he liked having another man in the bank when they were closing. As many people had seen these comings and goings of Norm, no one was concerned on this night either.

After the front door was locked, Norm indicated he would go to the back door to ensure it was double-locked. He had done this for Steven several times. This time, however, he let the rest of his group into the bank. They all wore masks. When the men returned to the front, a gun was pointed at Steven, and he was told to put all the money into bags. A gun was also pointed at Norm so neither of the other two would know he was in on the robbery. The other men left quickly out the back door and headed north at a trot on their horses and off the main road. They had put the money in their saddlebags so it was not visible to others as they passed. Norm instructed Steven and Beth to go get help, and he would follow the robbers and track them down. When the six meet up at the agreed to rendezvous, they were then ready for the second part of the plan.

Michael, Jonathan, and the other three men, Frank, Mitch, and Charlie, left within minutes of Andrew. They could tell they were going to the city, so they took a slightly different route. Michael, Frank, and Charlie entered the hotel and saw the group eating. Jonathan could not enter as Andrew would recognize him immediately, so Mitch stayed with him. Frank left just before Andrew's group finished eating to meet up with Jonathan. Michael and Jonathan thought the group would rob the bank but wasn't sure how. They saw Norm leave the hotel and head across the street to the bank, so Jonathan, Mitch, and Frank led their horses behind the bank and into a group of trees. After Andrew and the rest of the men exited the hotel, Michael and Charlie also left, leaving enough distance as not to be noticed. When the first group mounted their horses and took Norm's by the reins, they headed toward the back of the bank. Michael and Charlie did the same. The pair were able to flank the group and meet up with Jonathan and Frank in the trees. They saw Norm let Andrew and the other in and that they were wearing masks. Michael knew that it would not go well if they cornered these men in the bank; they were outnumbered and civilians may get hurt. They would wait until they had the advantage and no one could get caught in the crossfire.

The five saw Andrew and four of the men leave the bank, place the bags in their saddlebags, and head north. Norm came out a few minutes later going the same way. Charlie entered the bank to ensure on one was hurt and said he would catch up with them. Michael, Jonathan, Mitch, and Frank followed the others. By the time Charlie caught up, the robbers had entered a small clearing. Then they dismounted and started to walk east through the woods. Michael asked Jonathan if he knew what they could be doing. Jonathan knew of a plantation owner named Clement who lived in that direction. It was rumored that he kept all his money in the house. Michael wanted to know if they could get to the house first. Jonathan replied yes, and the five rode out to head off another robbery.

Chapter 32

The Union soldiers reached the Clement Plantation well before the Rebel 6 gang. They approached the front door with Jonathan saying he thought it would be better if he did the talking as Michael sounded too Northern. Michael chuckled and agreed. They knocked, and a male Negro answered the door.

Jonathan asked, "May we speak to the master of the house?" The Negro led them to Mr. Joseph Clement. Jonathan spoke in his most Southern drawl. "Sir, my name is John Johnson. I am the son of John Johnson Sr., who owns the Johnson Plantation south of Vicksburg. May we have a few minutes of your time?"

"What do you men want?" Joseph Clement said in an abrupt voice. He was not known to be a pleasant man.

"We are part of a group searching for former Southern soldiers doing harm to rich Southern civilians for money and killing northerners in the South," Jonathan responded. "We have information that a gang known as the Rebel 6 are heading here right now to rob you. We would like to prevent that with your help."

Joseph said, "You mean you are from the United States government. I don't need yours or anyone's help to protect myself. Go away."

Michael stepped forward. "Sir, these men are very dangerous and have actually killed many people including children. They should be here very soon."

Joseph said, "I told you no. If you want to watch outside, you just do that." Then he motioned them to go. Both Michael and

Jonathan started to try and convince him otherwise, but Joseph just turned and left the room.

As all the men started for the door, they heard a scream from the rear of the house. All the men lifted their guns and spread out. Michael pointed for two of them to go to the left, and he and Jonathan went right and Mitch was to stay put as backup. There were more voices, and they could clearly hear Andrew talking to Joseph Clement. Then there was shouting, and a shriek, and then silence. As the Union soldiers reached the room with all the noise, what they saw was startling.

There was George Wallace with one hand holding the hair of Joseph's wife and the other with a bloody knife that had just cut her throat. Joseph was down on his knees, crying, saying, "Please stop. Don't hurt anyone else. I will give you the money."

Michael and his men all pointed their guns, saying, "Drop your weapons!!"

Next, Andrew and Jonathan eyed each other, Jonathan with questioning eyes and Andrew with hatred in his. Jonathan said, "Andrew, stop. This must stop. Please don't make me shoot you."

Andrew laughed. "Brother, you are so naïve. The Northerners need to die, and the rich need to pay for not helping with our cause. You can try to shoot me, but it is more likely you will die in the process."

There was silence then shooting, yelling, knives gouging, fists flying, and when it was all done, everyone was either injured or dead. Of the Union soldiers, Frank and Mitch were dead, Charlie was bleeding badly, and Jonathan had a gash across his chest. Michael had a few stab wounds in his right arm, left leg, and his back. Of the Rebel 6 gang, George and Red were dead, Andrew and Simon were near death, and the other two were moaning on the floor. Joseph had stayed in the room, and he too was injured but not seriously.

Jonathan went and knelt by Andrew. "Hold on, brother. Please don't die… I love you and wish things were different. What happened to you?"

Andrew spoke weakly. "I saw too much. I learned to hate, hate them all. There is nothing left inside me, brother, but hate. Take care of Mother. Don't tell them if you can."

His voice had grown even softer. He squeezed Jonathan's hand, his eyes closed, and then…he was gone. Jonathan held him close, crying silently, praying God could forgive Andrew. War was such an evil thing. There were really never any true winners.

Other members of the Clements household were now in the back parlor with all the men. Michael asked the Negro men to remove all the weapons and tie the remaining gang members' hands together. He then asked that the wounded be tended to, especially Jonathan and Charlie. This was one night no one in this house would ever forget.

A member of the Clement house went into Vicksburg to seek more help. Upon the arrival of five more police officers and a doctor, the dead were removed, and the wounded were allowed to stay at least for a couple of days there in the house. One of the officers was to always remain with the three gang members still alive. Their wounds were serious, but they might recover.

Three days after the incident, all the wounded were moved. The gang members, Norm, Simon, and Mickey, and Union member Charlie were taken to the hospital in Vicksburg, and Michael and Jonathan returned to the plantation. Eventually, Simon also died from his injuries, and Norm and Mickey would probably recover and stand trial. Michael injuries were stitched as were Jonathan's, but Jonathan's would require a little more bed rest before he would be going anywhere.

Mother, Emma, and Margaret tended to Jonathan to the point he couldn't wait to get out of that bed. Although he secretly enjoyed the attention, it was getting irritating. The doctor had stopped by and said that he could get out of bed tomorrow but not to do anything strenuous for at least a week.

Charlie was also brought to the plantation. His right arm had suffered three deep slashes, and it wasn't clear if he would retain the complete use of that arm. Hamilton had been talking to him and thought he had some ideas if his arm didn't fully recover. Charlie and Hamilton were developing a good friendship.

Father and Mother planned the funeral for their son Andrew. Neither Michael nor Jonathan would go into details about what had happened but did need to address his actions. They gave only enough information to Father as necessary and knew he would draw the correct conclusions. They never wanted to give any details.

The funeral was held at the house with only close family and friends in attendance. He was buried in the family cemetery with his Confederate uniform on. It was a very sad day, but Father, Michael, and Jonathan knew that this was inevitable based on how he and his men had behaved.

Chapter 33

Bella and Michael had spent hours each of the next few days walking and talking, sneaking in kisses and what Marcus would call making "goo-goo" eyes at each other. Michael had also spent time walking the grounds with Father. They talked about the working of the plantations and what he and Jonathan were going to do in the future. Father said that his primary concern was the security and happiness of his daughter.

Another week passed when Michael received new orders since the Rebel 6 were no longer at large. Michael had instructions to go to Washington, DC, for a new position opening up. He was to head up the selection and training of a new type of unit in the Army. They would be the unit to handle very dangerous situations, similar to the Rebel 6 gang. Years later, this would become known as the Army Green Berets. He would be able to select his own staff. Michael shared this information with Jonathan, and they both were excited about the possibilities. Now…Michael was going to have to get things with Bella on the move.

Michael asked to talk to John Senior, or Father, that evening. So shortly after teatime, the two men entered the library.

Michael tried not to appear nervous. "Sir, as I stated the first day we met, I would like to marry your daughter, Bella. I love her very much and want to give her the best I can. I received new orders today to go to Washington, DC. They want me to head up a new unit with specialized training for more dangerous missions. I will be taking Jonathan with me, but more importantly, I would like Bella by my side."

John smiled, saying, "Now that I have gotten a chance to know you, it is clear you will take excellent care of my Bella, and she appears to love you too. This new unit you described, will you and Jonathan be in more danger than most Army officers?"

"Sir, I do not know yet, but I will make sure she is always safe," Michael said.

John stood and said, "You and Bella have my blessing to wed. And you can call me John." Michael's face lit up, then John continued, "Michael, here in the South, we still like to give a dowry when a young lady weds. I do not have the wealth I did before the war, but I would like to give you $500 for her dowry."

Michael also stood and replied, "Sir, John, that is very generous, but it is not necessary." But Michael saw the look on John's face. So he continued, "But if it is important to you, then I am happy for your daughter to take it with her."

The men shook hands, and then they both left the room smiling.

Bella and Mother were standing nearby as they knew what this conservation was all about. When they saw the two men smiling, the two ladies started jumping up and down and laughing giddily. Bella was getting married. They all walked back into the parlor and announced the news. Hugs, kisses, and handshakes were everywhere. The cutest was watching Marcus walk up to Michael and extend his hand like he saw Jonathan do. Michael grabbed it firmly and shook with Marcus saying, "Congratulations, welcome to the family."

The next morning, Michael and Bella walked to the Japanese garden to talk about the future. Michael started, "My dear Bella, are you all right with going to Washington, DC, with me? We may not stay there as training is likely to take place at some sort of fort or base location."

"I will go wherever you go. This is my chance to see other parts of the country. Will we get married here then leave together? And how soon?"

Michael smiled broadly. "You are so precious. We will need to leave soon. Do you think you and your mother can plan a ceremony to happen within the next ten days? If so, I will send word that I will be in DC in two to three weeks. How does that sound?"

"Yes" was all that came out. Then Michael kissed her, noticing that she was becoming a very good kisser. He couldn't wait for them to be married. He also knew it would need to take their lovemaking slowly and teach her. He definitely did not want to scare her.

Chapter 34

Mother and Bella spent the next five days going crazy. Bella needed a dress. Guests needed to be invited, food prepared, and decorations set. It was decided that Bella would wear her mother's wedding dress. A seamstress in Vicksburg came out to the house. They discussed the few changes they wanted to make so it would be unique for Bella and complement her coloring.

Next were the invitations. They were not inviting a lot of people, just close friends. They had some of the workers deliver them. Former slaves Kai and Georgia were very talented at arranging flowers. Mother had worked with them to develop their skills. Mother walked them through the gardens and pointed out the flowers she wanted to use. They won't be able to cut the flowers any earlier than two days prior to the wedding. Mother spent half a day talking to Emma planning the food they would have and when to serve them. Father did have one important task: He needed to talk to the local preacher about coming out to perform the ceremony.

Mother also had to review the clothes each of her other children were going to wear in addition to herself. Michael and Jonathan were both going to wear their dress uniforms. Father thought but dismissed the idea of wearing his Confederate uniform. Instead, he would wear his black suit. He thought of Andrew and how he wished his family could be whole again, but that was not going to happen. Michael, however, would make a great addition to the family. Maybe now Jonathan would start looking for a wife.

The day finally came for the wedding. The ceremony was held in the foyer. This way, everyone could see John walk Bella down the stairs. She looked so gorgeous. Her white satin dress had lace at the neckline and sleeves. There was a royal-blue ribbon at her waist and a few royal-blue orchids with a white rose and baby's breath attached to a comb in her hair to hold her veil in place. As she was much taller than her mother, a lace overlay was placed to lengthen the skirt. As Bella did not like hoops and the dress wasn't as wide as needed, she wore three petticoats to fill out the dress. Bella's mother presented her with a beautiful pearl necklace that belonged to her grandmother Johnson. Bella had never had a chance to meet her grandmother as she had died before Bella was born, but she had heard many stories. Father would say she was a feisty lady with a very determined mind and that Bella reminded him of his mother. She wore her white boots so she would be taller to dance with Michael. Mother cried as she watched her husband and daughter descend the staircase.

Bella barely remembered what she was saying or doing; it all seemed a blur, one beautiful, exquisite dream she never wanted to wake up from. She knew they danced and laughed; she thought she ate something, and then it was time to leave. Father and Mother decided to reopen Uncle Edwin's house a few months ago. They had changed the decor and furniture, painted or repapered the walls, and brought the outside appearance to a state that was truly enviable. They were going to rent the house, but as it had just been finished, there was no one in it yet. They wanted the new couple to be able to spend their first night alone. In the morning, Emma would go over to prepare them a great breakfast. It could wait until after the family's breakfast as they did not expect the newlyweds to be up early.

Chapter 35

Bella and Michael were taken down to the house in the small carriage, which was also decorated with blue and white carnations. Kai and Georgia made up scented flower arrangements to create a peaceful feel as they walked inside the redecorated house. They sat down and talked for a few minutes until Michael thought Bella was ready to go upstairs. As they climbed the steps, Michael held up her dress so she wouldn't trip while moving. Once at the top, he released her dress, and they moved to the master bedroom. Earlier that day, Mother and Ellie had brought over some clothes for tomorrow and some delicate nightwear for Bella for that night. Bella now realized she was very nervous; she had no idea what she was supposed to do.

Michael approached Bella from behind and placed his hands on her waist, whispering in her ear. Then he gently moved her hair so he could kiss her from her tender white shoulder and up along to her neck. They could both feel the shiver that ran up Bella's spine. *This feels amazing*, she thought. Next, Michael removed the flowered comb in her blond hair and all the pins holding the curls in place. He then ran his fingers through her hair to loosen it to its full length. He released the wide blue ribbon around her waist that was in a bow at the back of her dress just above her tiny round derriere.

Michael gently turned Bella around asking her to remove his jacket…slowly and to be sure to glide her hands along his arms. She did as directed, starting to enjoy this. Next, she was to unbutton his shirt starting from the top and moving to the bottom by pulling his shirt out from his pants. As Bella unfastened each button, she started to see the curly dark hair on his chest. The more buttons she released, the more hair she saw. She had never been this close to a man or a hairy chest. She wanted to run her fingers through this hair. Bella hesitated then touched his chest and moved her fingers in little circles through the rough, curly hair. She could see Michael react to her touch.

Michael then sat down in the nearest chair, a tall-back armed chair with red and gold fabric, and removed his tall black shiny boots and his socks. Then he stood, lifted Bella, and turned around to place her in the chair. Michael removed her boots, noticing how much smaller they were compared to his. As he ran his hands up her right leg to reach the garter holding her stocking in place, Bella's heart was beating so fast she thought it would explode. Michael rolled the stocking down to her ankle and slid it off. Then he repeated on the next leg. By this time, the ache they both felt for each other was immense.

Michael had Bella stand and unbuttoned her bodice, revealing the tops of her sweet breasts. His finger traced from her left shoulder down along the strap of the camisole, across its top, and up the right shoulder. Bella could feel her nipples harden. Bella removed Michael's shirt and unfastened her own skirt and let it slip down to the floor. She reached for Michael's hand as she stepped over it. She removed the top petticoat and waited.

Michael helped her remove the next two petticoats. Then he looked at all the clothes she still had on, asking why women wore so many layers. Bella shrugged, and they both gave a little chuckle. She still had on her camisole, corset, chemise (undershirt), and drawers (linen underpants). Michael unbuckled his belt and pulled it from its loops and unbuttoned the top of his pants. Bella lifted her camisole over her head and let Michael untie the corset from behind. That was one piece of clothing a woman could not remove on her own.

He led her to the bed, pulled back the soft navy-colored coverlet, and sat down upon the white satin sheets. Michael then reached for her to get close to him, picked up her hands, and placed them on his face. He reached for her again and this time kissed her gently. The kisses grew quicker and deeper, and they yearned for each other.

ANNABELLA'S STORY

Michael rolled them onto the middle of the bed. The touching and kissing continued with intensity. Michael stopped and removed his pants and Bella's chemise. Michael caressed her breasts and guided her hand to his nether region. Bella's body felt an ache she had never known. She whispered for him to continue as she also did.

Finally, all the clothes were on the floor. Bella and Michael were embroiled in passionate lovemaking. He continued to be gentle with her at first until she begged him for more. They slept embraced in each other's arms; actually, their entire bodies were intertwined. They awoke, more lovemaking, and slept again. This continued until Bella was too tired to do anything but rest in blissful joy.

The next morning, Michael awoke first to the morning sunlight cascading through the window. He raised on one elbow to look at his new wife. He smiled and was at peace for the first time in his life. He washed, dressed quietly, and proceeded down the stairs so as not to awake Bella. They had been very busy last night, and she needed her rest as he expected many similar nights.

Michael walked into the kitchen to see if Emma had arrived to prepare their first breakfast together. Emma glanced up at Michael as he entered the room. The smile on his face said all she needed to know.

Emma inquired, "Is Ms. Bella still sleep'ng?"

Michael replied, "She is. There was little sleeping last night."

Emma smiled with a giggle. "I 'member, I 'member. You want someth'ng till Ms. Bella wakes?"

"I would if you don't mind. I am pretty famished," Michael said.

Emma smiled again and handed him some corn bread with some sausage then went to pour him a cup of coffee. Michael thanked her and went out on the front porch to enjoy the morning air.

A short time later, Bella came down in her nightgown and robe. Michael was back inside the house examining all the fine pieces now in place. He liked this house; it was the perfect size for a young family. He surprised himself by already thinking of a house and children. This made him smile; he sure was smiling a lot in the past few weeks.

Bella said, "Good morning, my dear husband," walking a little slowly as she was somewhat sore.

"Good morning, my dear wife. Would you like to share a meal with me? Emma has been preparing some wonderful dishes for our first breakfast." Emma nodded and walked over to Michael, and the two proceeded to the dining room. There they enjoyed a very tasty meal, talking to each other about what was going to happen next.

The newlyweds spent the day together walking and talking. They did not return to the plantation house until teatime. The family greeted them, and they enjoyed a fun evening in each other's company. Bella and Michael let everyone know they would be leaving in two days for Washington, DC. Jonathan spoke up to say he too was going to DC. Jonathan had already talked to his father about the opportunity presented to Michael and that he had been asked to be on Michael's staff.

The next day was spent packing for the trip. Michael warned Bella to pack sparingly as she could only take two bags with her. After they were settled and knew where they would be ultimately stationed, then she could send for the rest of her things. Finally, he let her know she would be allowed to use her dowry as she wished. Mother and Bella spend a few hours reviewing which items would be sent upon her request.

The morning of their departure was full of anxiety and hopefulness. Hugs and kisses were given to all, and the three mounted their horses. Bella decided to take Fancy as she was now her favorite horse. The future held so many possibilities for all members of the Johnson family and the newlyweds themselves. As Michael, Bella, and Jonathan rode their horses at a slow walk, they all turned to look one more time at their family and the grand house of the plantation. They vowed to return; it was just a question of when…

Note of Interest

Of the 60 biggest Civil War battles,

- 55 had West Point grads commanding both sides, and
- 5 had West Point grads commanding one side.

About the Author

Mary Jo grew up in Columbus, Ohio, the oldest of six children. She was very active in sports and finished high school as the valedictorian of her senior class. She married and attended Ohio State University. After three years, she had her first son, left college to take care of him, and worked part-time. Her second son was born eighteen months later. Then she finished her degree and received a BS in accounting. Mary Jo worked from 1983 to 2013 in the accounting field with her last position as controller of a company in Louisville, Kentucky. She then returned to Columbus, Ohio, and purchased a pottery store and helped out her parents. Upon their deaths in 2016 and 2017, she moved into her own condo. COVID-19 forced the end of her business in 2020. Due to a hereditary medical condition, she qualified for disability in December 2020. She now lives with her eight-pound Maltese, Frank, and finds things to keep her from being bored. After spending fifteen months writing a family journal, she found she liked doing research and writing. This is her first story.

Printed in the USA
CPSIA information can be obtained
at www.ICGtesting.com
LVHW091801260524
781366LV00002B/239